Contents

1

Gizzmo Gets Going

Gizzmo hung the framed certificate on the wall of his little office and stepped back proudly.

Moonistry of Defence

This is to certify that
GIZZMO R. LEWIS
has achieved the minimum standard
necessary to qualify as a
SECRET AGENT
for secret operations concerned with the
security of the planet Sigma–6.
And he'd better not tell anyone
about this because
it's supposed to be a secret.

Signed: **The General**

Gizzmo sat down at his little desk.

He stood up, checked that the certificate was hanging perfectly straight, then sat down again.

He checked the drawers of his desk. Empty. You couldn't get much more secret than that!

He stood up again and had another look at the

certificate. Signed by The General himself! In his own footwriting! Gizzmo could scarcely believe it.

His first morning as a newly-qualified secret agent.

What would his first job be?

He sat down at his desk and waited for something to happen.

Something was about to.

Not far away, in his headquarters deep beneath the surface of Sigma–6, The General was sitting at his own desk. He had a problem.

'I've got a problem, BrainBox,' he said. 'I need answers.'

The square box perched on The General's desk glowed, flickered, and then made a yawning noise. 'And is one correct in supposing, General, that you are about to ask one for the answers you need?'

'Yes, one is,' growled The General, 'because you're a computer, BrainBox, and computers are supposed to have all the answers.'

'True,' said the box. 'It's just that your questions are always so frightfully easy. What is it this time, then? That travel-capsule you shoot around in costing too much is it? If I've told you once I've told you a zillion times General, get something more economical. A top-of-the-range Zingdinger Convertible indeed! I don't suppose the thing does more than a couple of light-seconds to the gallon. . . .'

'No, this is what I'm unhappy about,' snapped The General. He waved a sheet of paper in front of the computer's vision sensors. 'This letter.'

'Mmm. Looks official.'

'It's more than official, BrainBox,' said The General. 'It's from . . .' he snapped smartly to attention '. . . the Prime Moonister herself! So listen.'

'I'm all ears, General.'

'No you're not, you're all brain. That's the only reason I put up with your nagging. Now then, the Prime Moonister has decided to rid Sigma–6 of noise pollution. A whole new set of Noise Laws are going to be introduced. For instance, it will be a crime to turn your telewhatson up so loud that it annoys the people next door. It will also be an offence to use one of those awful personal blareos in a public place.'

'Really?'

'Yes. Even to be found carrying the batteries will mean . . .'

'Don't tell me, don't tell me,' cried BrainBox, 'you get charged!'

'All those found guilty of noise crimes,' continued The General, raising his voice, 'will be banished to a primitive, far-away planet until they learn to be a bit quieter.'

'Ah. A case of hear today, gone tomorrow.'

The General had had enough. He waved the Prime Moonister's letter again and bellowed at the top of his voice, 'AND *THAT* IS WHY I'VE GOT A PROBLEM!'

'Why? Starting with Generals who shout too loud are they?' asked the computer.

'Give me strength,' moaned The General. 'My problem, BrainBox, is that the Prime Moonister wants a secret agent to land on this planet and find out what sort of resistance there'd be if we tried to take it over.'

BrainBox sighed again. It was a hard life dealing with dimbos when one was a super-brain. 'So why is that a problem, General?'

'Because my secret agents joined up for excitement, that's why, not to go looking around primitive far-away planets. Talk about boring. Who in their right mind is going to want to do this job?'

'At last!' cried BrainBox. 'A decent question.' The computer flickered brilliantly. 'The answer,' it said almost at once, 'is somebody who is *awfully* keen and *awfully* enthusiastic. Somebody who won't care about being sent to a nasty, boring little planet. In other words, General, a secret agent who is *awfully* . . . new.'

'Brilliant!' cried The General. He frowned. 'But have we got anybody like that? Search your records, BrainBox.'

'One already has, General. And we have. His name is . . .'

'Gizzmo Lewis at your service, General!'

Gizzmo stepped into The General's office and saluted smartly. His first job! Great! What would it be? Where would it be?

'Now then, Lewis,' said The General. 'I need you to go on a mission. An important mission. A really important mission. Got that?'

Mission. Important mission. Really important mission. Phew! 'Got it. Yes, sir, General sir.'

4

'You have been specially selected,' said The General. 'By computer,' he added significantly.

'Thank you, thank you,' said BrainBox. 'It was nothing.'

'Who said that?' said Gizzmo. The voice seemed to have come from nowhere. He looked around. Nothing. Only when BrainBox called, 'Cooeee!' and flickered brightly, did Gizzmo notice the computer sitting on The General's desk.

'What on Sigma is it?' said Gizzmo.

'Its name is BrainBox,' said The General. 'Because . . .'

'One is box-shaped,' interrupted the computer, 'and awfully, awfully clever. Would you like one to give you a demonstration?'

'No,' snapped The General, 'one would not.' He turned to Gizzmo. 'Now then Lewis. Do you think you can do it, this really important mission?'

'Yes, General!' said Gizzmo. A thought struck him. 'Er . . . what is it, exactly?'

The General answered in a low whisper. 'Your mission, Lewis, is to land on a far-away planet and report back on their defensive capabilities. Understand that?'

Far-away planet. Defensive capabilities. Right. Gizzmo nodded.

'Now it's only fair to warn you, Lewis, this planet is inhabited by very ugly-looking creatures. Tell him about them, BrainBox.'

'The creatures are, for the most part, of a binary construction, being to all intents and purposes symmetrical about a vertical axis.'

'Pardon?' said Gizzmo.

BrainBox tutted. 'They stand upright and

they've got two of nearly everything. Two arms, two legs, two feet, two eyes, two ears . . .'

'Told you they were ugly, didn't I?' said The General.

'Wh- wh- what's the name of this planet?' stammered Gizzmo.

'Dear me,' said BrainBox. 'Don't they teach you secret agents anything? There's only one place in the whole universe inhabited by ghastly creatures like that. The planet Earth.'

'That's where you're going, Lewis,' said The General. 'The planet Earth! Exciting, eh? Not every agent gets a chance like this so early in his career. Right then. Ready?'

Gizzmo took a deep breath. 'Yes sir, General, sir.'

'Come on, then,' said The General. He picked up BrainBox with two hands and opened his office door with the other. 'Your spacecraft awaits you. This way.'

'What is it?' asked Gizzmo. The spacecraft looked unlike anything he'd ever seen before.

The General looked pleased. 'Fooled you, eh? Thought it would. Well, believe it or not Lewis, this is a standard-issue, Mark 2 Whereami Orbital Outing Space-Hopper.'

'A Mark 2 WOOSH?' gasped Gizzmo. 'But it doesn't look . . .'

'Anything like a WOOSH? Wrong, Lewis.' The General whipped open one of the Space-Hopper's doors. 'Inside, as you can see, it looks just like a WOOSH because it *is* a WOOSH. But on the out-

6

side – correct, it doesn't look like a WOOSH. And why?'

'I don't know, General.'

'Because it isn't meant to look like one. It looks like what it *is* meant to look like. An earth-vehicle!'

Gizzmo gawped at the long low body, with its four round things at each corner and the funny little figure perched on the front. 'An earth-vehicle?' he said. 'You mean they fly around in these?'

'Not fly,' said The General. 'Roll. Hence its name . . .'

'Rolls-Royce,' said BrainBox. 'A wonderful camouflage selected by wonderful me. Land this spacecraft anywhere on Earth, Lewis, and it will instantly become part of the scenery. The earth-creatures will have no idea you're amongst them.'

Gizzmo found it hard to believe that such a ridiculous-looking object could become part of any scenery anywhere but, if it was true, then he was impressed.

'One more thing before you go,' said The General. He took a small round container from his pocket and handed it to Gizzmo. 'Here. You'll need these.'

Carefully, Gizzmo took hold of the container. Could it be? No, surely not. He shook it gently. Inside, something rattled. Lots of something.

Could it really be? He peeped inside. It was! Was it?

'Are they . . . really . . . are they?'

'Transformation tablets?' said The General, 'yes Lewis, they are.'

7

So it was true. Transformation tablets really did exist. 'Cor!' said Gizzmo.

'Follow the instructions on the box, Lewis,' said The General, 'and you can take on the appearance of any known earth-creature. But guard those tablets carefully. The formula is top secret. Only an earful of Sigmatians know it.'

'Including oneself, naturally,' said BrainBox, 'one having been the super-brain that devised the formula in the first place.'

'Ye- yes, sir,' said Gizzmo.

He tucked the box of transformation tablets into his tunic pocket and stepped through the door of the Rolls-Royce. Amazing! Inside it *was* just like a standard-issue Mark 2 WOOSH. He slipped into the padded driver's seat.

'Right then,' said The General. 'Anything else you want to know before you go?'

Gizzmo thought hard. 'Er . . . well . . . there is one thing, General.'

'Yes? Yes?'

'You . . . er . . . don't know the way to Earth, do you?'

BrainBox didn't give The General a chance. 'Straight up,' said the computer immediately, 'until you reach the Intergalactic-13 East. Follow that until you reach Exit 41239 signposted Milky Way. Then it's left at Pluto, onto the Neptune fly-over, sharp right at Uranus, round the Saturn ring road, straight past Jupiter and it's first on the left after Mars. Easy.'

'Got that, Lewis?'

'I – I think so, General. Intergalactic-13 East

8

until I get to Exit 39142 signposted Murky Way . . .'

'Milky Way,' tutted BrainBox, 'Exit 41239.'

'Left at Pluto, right at Neptune, stay on Saturn road for a bit . . .'

'Left at Pluto, onto the Neptune flyover, sharp right at Uranus, round the Saturn ring road,' corrected BrainBox. 'Oh it's hopeless, General. He'll never get there.'

'Hmmm,' said The General thoughtfully. 'Maybe Lewis here needs some help.'

'If you ask me, Lewis here needs another brain.'

'Another brain, eh? Do you know, BrainBox, for once I couldn't agree with you more. Right, in you get then.' And in one smooth action, The General moved the computer from under his arm and tossed it on to the passenger seat beside Gizzmo.

'Not me!' wailed BrainBox, 'I didn't mean me! I don't want to go! I'll miss you! You'll miss me!'

'Oh, I will,' said The General, 'no nagging, no interruptions, no awful jokes . . . I don't know how I'll manage.'

'Welcome aboard BrainBox,' said Gizzmo as the Space-Hopper's door slammed shut.

'Don't you welcome me,' snarled the computer. 'I don't want to go! I want to get out!'

'Good luck!' yelled The General.

'I get car sick! I get headaches!!'

'Oh, keep your hair on,' said Gizzmo. 'Earth here we come!'

2
No Exit

It was morning break at St Arthur's High School. Various activities were in progress.

Out by the entrance a couple of the more creative pupils were painting. They worked swiftly. A big blob here, a couple of dabs there, and it was done. By the time the school caretaker chased them off it was too late. A new saint had been created. The school sign-board now read *St Thugs High School*.

'Half a mind to leave it,' muttered Dobson, the caretaker, as he trudged off to find a bucket and a mop.

Behind him, things were happening in the playground to explain why he thought that way.

A group of older boys were trying to persuade a first-former to take part in their football match. The first-former was trying to persuade the older boys that he wouldn't roll very well and they'd do much better to find a football instead.

Half-a-dozen girls with collecting tins were roaming the playground, looking for customers.

'We're collecting for somebody who's going into hospital tomorrow.'

'Who?'

'You, if you don't put something in this collection.'

Perched elegantly on her usual wall, Ros Price tutted at the sight of such behaviour. Committing acts of violence against one's fellow pupils was not Ros's style at all. Certainly not. She had Masher to do that sort of thing for her.

'Masher . . .' she said.

The big boy at her side looked up in adoration. 'Yes, Ros?'

Ros smiled sweetly. 'Masher, I stayed over long in my boudoir this morning and my mater wouldn't let me have any breakfast, the ratbag. Do something to remedy the situation, would you?'

Masher's look of adoration faded momentarily. 'Eh?' he said.

'I feel peckish, Masher.'

'Peckish?' said Masher, frowning in concentration. He thought carefully. His beloved had spoken to him and he wanted to make sure he'd understood fully. 'Hungry, you mean?'

'Hungry!' yelled Ros as her patience snapped. 'Me guts think me throat's been cut – that sort of hungry!'

Masher nodded his head slowly. 'Oh. Hungry. Right.'

Ros smiled sweetly. 'If you were a gentleman, Dudley McTurk, you'd get me something to eat.'

'I am a gentleman, Ros. Whajja want?'

'Mmm . . . something delicate, I think.' She pursed her lips, sending a shiver down Masher's lengthy spine. 'Something to suit my discriminating palate. Something like . . . ooh . . . a bag of prawn cocktail crisps.'

Masher jumped down from the wall, producing

a few more cracks in the school's crumbling playground as he landed.

'Right,' he said. 'Prawn cocktail crisps it is.'

He strode off, his trousers flapping above his
ankles and the cuffs of his blazer halfway up
his arms. Most boys took a year to outgrow their
clothes. Masher seemed able to do it in a fortnight.
Suddenly he stopped, turned and strode back.

'Where am I going to get prawn cocktail crisps,
Ros?'

Ros sighed. This was all too much. Why were
good slaves so difficult to come by nowadays?

She aimed a slim index finger. 'There, Masher.
Snotty Simkins has just got a packet out.'

Masher's face lit up. This was a message he
could understand. More than that, it was a chance
to use the one real talent he possessed. 'Say no
more Ros. Your wish is my whatsit.'

Pulling a specially-baked (regulo 5 for a whole
weekend) conker from his pocket, Masher took
aim.

Shweeee-conkk!

'Aaagh!' screamed Simkins, as the bullet-hard
missile cracked him on the wrist and sent the
crisp packet flying from his hand like the gun from
a slow-on-the-draw cowboy.

Masher strolled across, picked up the crisps,
and brought them proudly back to their new
owner.

'Thank you, my man,' said Ros.

But the sight of his favourite snack being
snatched had stirred the frightened Simkins into
a burst of bravado. 'Give me those back!' he yelled,

12

running up to where Ros had already popped the packet open.

'Get lost,' said Masher.

Simkins stayed. 'I mean it! If you don't give me them back I'll report you! Owww!'

'D'you reckon that was a good idea?' said Masher.

Ros popped a crisp into her mouth. 'A shade too much prawn and not quite enough cocktail,' she said 'but . . . yes, all things considered Masher, I would say that relieving Simkins of his crisps was a good idea.'

'No,' said Masher. He pointed over to where Simkins was now running round in circles, 'I mean, d'you think it was a good idea to stick your pen where you did?'

Ros looked mystified. 'Why ever not?'

'Well . . .' said Masher, searching for an impressive reason, '. . . you might need it for writing wiv.'

This was not an impressive reason. Ros looked down on him as though she were a queen addressing a particularly lowly subject.

'To write with, Masher? I think not.'

Masher was confused. 'But we do do writing at school. Don't we?'

'True,' said Ros 'but not today . . .' she snapped her fingers and Masher immediately fell to his knees. Slipping elegantly down from the wall using Masher's broad back as a stepping stone, she went on, '. . . today I am not in a writing mood. Today I am . . .'

'Just in a mood?' asked Masher as he struggled to his feet.

'In a reflective mood,' said Ros.

'How d'you mean?'

'I mean, Masher, that I feel like looking at my reflection in a mirror. A hairdresser's mirror to be precise.'

A bell jangled. Peace of sorts broke out as almost all the pupils of St Arthur's High School began to form themselves into lines. Only Ros and Masher didn't move. Masher didn't move because he wasn't going to move anywhere until Ros moved. And Ros didn't move because she had no intention of moving – not towards a classroom, anyway.

As the lines started to head for the school building, Ros spun on her heel.

'Where yer going?' called Masher.

'To have me hair done,' Ros answered over her shoulder. 'I am heading for the shopping centre, via the posterior exit.'

'Eh?' said Masher, loping dutifully behind.

'Out the back way! Come on!'

Ros knew the route as only a practised escapee could. Out of the playground and down alongside the kitchens where there was no chance of being caught. A fair chance of catching something nasty from the dustbins they had to dodge past, yes, but no chance of being caught.

From there, into the sports block, through the gymnasium and out again. No chance of being caught there either, not with the gym having been declared out of bounds until whoever stole the wall bars brought them back again.

It was as they dashed away from the empty sports block that they heard the gently spluttering sound overhead.

For once, Masher was the first to spot something.

'Whazzat?' he said, looking up at the strange object low in the sky.

Ros skidded to a halt. She looked up. 'It's . . . I don't know.'

'Well whatever it is, it's gonna land!' yelled Masher.

'No, it's going too fast.'

Now in normal circumstances Masher would have thought – he being a thicko and Ros being cool and smart and sophisticated – that she must be right and he must be wrong and, that being the case, he would have promptly shut his gob before she told him to. But these were not normal circumstances.

'It's gonna land, I tell you!' He pointed wildly towards the tall concrete building stuck on to the back of the shopping centre. 'On top of the multi-storey!'

Ros shook her head, coolly, smartly and with a fair amount of sophistication.

'Masher, are you at all conversant with the laws of aerodynamics?'

'Who?'

'Precisely. Then believe me when I say that that whatever-it-is is not going to land on top of the multi-storey car park.'

Hands on hips she stood and watched as the thing in the sky slowed, coughed a little, slowed a bit more and then finally dropped heavily downwards.

'It's landed!' yelled Masher. 'On top of the multi-storey!'

'What did I say!' screamed Ros, without any coolness at all. 'Come on!'

She hitched up her fashionable pencil-slim skirt and began to run . . . to run, in her excitement, straight into the one part of her escape route that needed just a teeny-weeny bit of caution . . . the part which led out through a gap in the school railings and past a small health food shop . . . a small health food shop that was very popular with a headmistress who didn't like the thought of what the school dinners dished up at St Arthur's would do to her already large and imposing figure . . . the large and imposing figure which, at the very moment that Ros and Masher reached the shop, stepped out into their path . . . the large and imposing figure of Miss Wilhemina 'Stony' Hart, MA, Headmistress of St Arthur's High School.

'Miss Price! McTurk! Good day to you both.'

'Stony!' cried Ros, skidding to halt. 'I mean . . . stone me, fancy meeting you here, Miss Hart.'

'Fancy indeed, Rosalind,' said Stony stonily. 'Now, don't tell me. Let me guess. McTurk and yourself, anxious not to be late for your next lesson, have decided to take a short cut. Through the shopping mall. Correct?'

'Yes, Miss Hart. I mean no, Miss Hart.'

'You, seem uncertain, Rosalind. How about you, McTurk?'

Masher cringed. He might be big for his age, but so was Stony. And as she was a lot older, that made her a lot bigger. 'Er . . . dunno, Miss.'

'Do you ever, McTurk?'

'Er . . . dunno, Miss,' repeated Masher.

16

'But, Miss Hart . . .' pleaded Ros. Here they were with a real bit of excitement to fill the day and all they'd got was Stony giving them a hard time. 'Didn't you see it, Miss Hart?' she said.

Stony looked down her nose, wrinkling it as though she'd just trodden in something nasty. 'Oh, I saw it all right.'

'You did?'

'Yes,' she snarled, 'two skivers nipping out the back way.'

'No, no,' said Ros, pointing. 'Up in the sky.'

Masher joined in. 'Yeh! It was one of those . . . a whajemercallit . . . a you-know!'

'He means a UFO,' said Ros.

'A UFO,' echoed Stony.

'Like a hang-glider it was!' said Masher, 'a massive hang-glider!'

'We saw it come down, Miss. On top of the multi-storey.'

'Ah,' said Stony. 'More of a bang-glider then.'

Ros could see they were getting nowhere. 'It's true!' she said. 'Don't you believe in UFOs Miss Hart?'

Stony's eyes narrowed. Above and around them swam a wild bush of grey, frizzy hair. She looked like a suspicious Brillo pad. 'Oh, yes,' she said, 'I believe in UFOs all right. Unpleasant Fleeing Objects. Like you two.'

'But . . .' began Ros.

'But . . .' said Masher.

'Silence!'

Ros and Masher took a step backwards. They'd been at St Arthur's long enough to know that arguing was pointless when their headmistress looked the way she did now. The end was nigh when you were faced by a grave-Stony. 'You will return to your classroom. And if you are not present for my mathematics lesson, your numbers will be up. Do I make myself clear?'

'Yes, Miss Hart,' mumbled Ros.

'Yes, Miss Hart,' said Masher, behind as usual.

'Good. Now go back the way you came.'

'But . . .'

'Go!!'

The headmistress watched sourly as Ros and Masher turned away. What had she done to deserve all this?

In her younger days she'd dreamed of being a high-flyer, in charge of a school of great standing. And what had she got? St Arthur's, where it was a wonder that the school was still standing at all.

Stony shook her head sadly. Talk about coming down to earth with a bump!

3

Space Invaders

Up on the top deck of the multi-storey car park, all was not well with two other high fliers who had come down to earth with a bump.

'My head,' groaned BrainBox, 'I landed on my head.'

'You're all head,' said Gizzmo. 'You couldn't land on anything else.'

The computer turned an angry shade of red. 'Well don't blame me if I can't think straight for a couple of days. When one gets one of one's headaches one is not answerable for one's answers. Didn't they teach you how to land a spaceship properly?'

'Me?' said Gizzmo. 'I thought *you* were doing the landing. I was looking out of the window.'

'Listen,' said BrainBox. 'I do the thinking, because I am a super-brain. You do the flying because you're a bird-brain.'

'Well, we're here anyway,' said Gizzmo. It was about time he started showing this computer who was boss, he decided. 'Call up The General on the telegroan and tell him we've arrived.'

With a sigh, the computer connected its circuits to the spaceship's inter-stellar communications system. The air was filled with brrr-brr noises, followed, moments later, by the sound of a familiar voice.

'General here! Who's there?'

'Us, General,' shouted Gizzmo, 'Gizzmo Lewis and BrainBox. We're here!'

'Here? You're not supposed to be here. You're supposed to be on your way to wherever I sent you.'

'But we are! We're here! We've arrived on Earth. Safe and sound.'

'Speak for yourself.' It was BrainBox. 'My head feels funny. Very, very funny.' The computer had gone a sickly shade of green.

The General wasn't interested. His thoughts were on more important matters than computers with a pain in the brain.

'Right, then. Have you spotted anything down there yet?' he said. 'Anything out of the ordinary?'

'Nothing at all,' squeaked BrainBox. 'Except stars. I'm seeing stars.'

'I . . . I'm not sure,' said Gizzmo nervously. 'I saw something out of the window just before we touched down.'

BrainBox blew an electronic raspberry. 'That was a touch-down? A thump-down, more like. My head!'

'Quiet BrainBox!' barked The General. 'Now, remember Lewis. You're looking for signs of a military capability. Anything to suggest the earth-creatures could put up a struggle when we take them over. So then, what have you seen?'

'A large flat area,' said Gizzmo. 'Like a parade ground.'

20

'A parade ground? What makes you think it was a parade ground?'

'It had earth-creatures on it. They were lining up, General.'

'Might be nothing,' said The General. 'Might not be military. They'd be in uniform if they were military.'

'Th- th- they *were* in uniform,' said Gizzmo.

'What!' The General's voice crackled with excitement. 'Did you see anything else?'

'A big sign,' said Gizzmo into the telegroan. He looked out of the Space-Hopper's window. 'I can just see it from where we are. I landed us on top of a high building you see,' he added, with a satisfied glance at BrainBox. For once the computer didn't answer back, just sat there looking unhappy.

'What does it say then, this sign?' asked The General.

'Just going to check, sir,' said Gizzmo crisply, 'through the old spynoculars.' He rummaged around under the dashboard and pulled out a tubular device which he pointed at the St Arthur's notice board.

'Well?' said The General. 'What does it say?'

' "High School",' said Gizzmo quietly.

The telegroan fell silent as the importance of this information sank in. 'High School, eh?' said The General finally. 'Hmmm. You know what this means, don't you?'

'No,' admitted Gizzmo.

'Neither do I,' said The General. 'Any ideas, BrainBox?'

'Soooo-rrrry?' said the computer, sounding like a tape that was running at the wrong speed.

J91, 915

Gizzmo looked at the computer. It had gone very pale. 'High School,' he said. 'What does it mean?'

BrainBox said nothing for a moment. Then, flickering madly, the computer blurted out in a squeaky voice, 'High . . . tall, very tall, very very tall, elevated, up in the air, off the ground, in the sky, sky-high.'

It paused, then started again.

'School . . . learning, training, find out what's going on, lessons, lessons, lessons, more lessons, loads of lessons, teach them a lesson . . .'

Gizzmo almost leapt out of his seat in excitement. 'High School!' he yelled down the telegroan, 'up-in-the-air training centre!'

'What?' said The General.

'Don't you get it General? High School . . . a place where they have lessons for up-in-the-air people.'

'Yes . . .'

'It must be a training camp for astronauts!'

The General was impressed. 'Good thinking, Lewis!' he barked. 'But . . . this is serious.'

'It is?'

'Of course it is. We were thinking of invading them. What if they're thinking of invading us?'

'Oh,' said Gizzmo. 'I see.'

'Are they friendly, Lewis?' barked The General. 'Can you tell if they're friendly?'

Gizzmo thought hard. He'd made a great start, no doubt about that. But this was awkward. Were they friendly? Maybe the sign-board would give him another clue. Eagerly he focussed his spynoculars on the lettering before 'High School'.

Now, had the secret agent from Sigma–6 landed

a bit later, after the school caretaker had finished cleaning up the notice board, he would have read a sparkling clean 'St Arthurs'.

On the other foot, if he'd landed a bit earlier, he would have read the graffiti-fied wording, 'St Thugs'.

As it was, Gizzmo read neither of these two because he'd landed at the very time that the St Arthur's caretaker, having done enough scrubbing to bring the Ar back into view, had decided to pop off for a refreshing cup of tea before turning the 'g' back into an 'r'.

So, what Gizzmo actually read was: 'St Arthugs'.

'Well?' crackled The General.

'There's a bit more on the sign-board,' said Gizzmo. Slowly he read out the letters. 'S.T.A.R.T.H.U.G.S.'

'Starthugs?' said The General. 'Starthugs?'

'Star thugs!' cried Gizzmo. He knew what a star was, but . . . 'What's a thug? BrainBox, do you know?'

The computer gave a big sigh, as though thinking was just too much effort. 'Thug,' it said, 'mean, rotten, nasty, obnoxious, goes round beating up people for fun . . .'

'Golly,' said Gizzmo. 'So a star thug is . . .'

'You don't have to spell it out!' yelled The General. 'And you've found a training camp for the creatures!'

Gizzmo's mind turned a few somersaults. He had. Yes, he had. Well!

'This is terrible!' wailed The General. 'Here we are thinking we're going to invade them and all the while they're getting ready to send up rockets full of these star thug creatures to invade us!'

'Er . . . well . . . yes, I suppose so.'

'Lewis,' said The General seriously, 'this is serious. These star thugs have got to be stopped.'

'Yes, sir!' answered Gizzmo. 'Er . . . who by?'

'You, Lewis! The future of Sigma–6 is in your hands. Only you can do it.'

'I can?'

'Well if you can't, you'd better not come back here. Under and out.'

'I don't feel well,' said BrainBox, as Gizzmo disconnected the telegroan. 'I want to go home.'

'Well you can't,' said Gizzmo. 'You heard The General. We've got a job to do.'

'We? We? "The future of Sigma–6 is in your hands," he said. It can't be in my hands, I haven't got any.'

'No, but you've got a super-brain . . .'

'And a super-headache,' moaned BrainBox.

'Together we can do it,' said Gizzmo with grim determination.

But how?

Gizzmo pulled a little blue book from his tunic pocket. It was his Sigma–6 Secret Service Handbook, presented to him on the day of his graduation as a secret agent. Surely this would give him some ideas? That was what the SSSSH was for, after all. That was what made it so hussssh-hussssh.

He flipped through the index. No sign of any

reference to 'thugs'. Nothing under 'high school', either.

Aha! 'Enemy'. Page 11, paragraph 14 (a). That might help. Gizzmo turned the pages quickly.

ENEMY

Know your enemy.
Better still, know what your enemy knows.
That way you'll have no trouble, y'know.

Yes, that was it. He had to infiltrate the enemy camp. Find out what they were planning, without them knowing who he was. But to do that he needed – a disguise.

Gizzmo undid the box of transformation tablets The General had given him. The tablets were all different colours. Each one had different lettering stamped on it. Gizzmo poked through them.

'Aha!' He pulled one out. It was a blue tablet, marked 'schoolboy'. The star thugs' training camp was called a school, wasn't it? So a schoolboy must be . . . well, Gizzmo wasn't sure what a schoolboy must be – but, whatever it was, it sounded hopeful.

'Here goes,' he muttered.

The transformation tablet went down with a gulp.

For a moment Gizzmo felt nothing.

Then, suddenly, bits of him started moving. Things began to stretch, first one way, then the other.

His insides jiggled. His outsides juggled.

Some parts of him grew bigger. Some parts of

him grew smaller. Some parts of him disappeared altogether.

It felt as if he had a family of pet gerbils scampering around inside his tunic.

'How do I look, BrainBox?' said Gizzmo when things finally stopped moving.

'As horrible as I feel,' said the computer.

Anxiously, Gizzmo looked down at his new shape. BrainBox was right. He *did* look horrible. Just like a star thug, in fact. The transformation tablet had worked!

Now for the next bit. He lifted BrainBox out of the Space-Hopper and shut the door.

'Where are you taking me? Where are we going?'

'To the Star Thugs High School,' said Gizzmo grimly.

'One doesn't want to go to school,' whined Brain-Box. 'One doesn't feel well. I'll print you out a sick-note.'

'No excuses, BrainBox,' said Gizzmo grimly. 'The future of Sigma—6 is at stake.'

And with that he tucked the computer under his arm and marched boldly for the door marked Exit.

4

Know Trouble

Slowly, carefully, Gizzmo made his way towards the star thugs training camp.

Slowly, because he was still getting used to the strange earth body that the transformation tablet had given him.

And carefully, because he was worried about guards. Top secret training camps always had guards on the front gate.

The strip of land which ran in front of the star thugs camp had earth-vehicles positioned all the way along it. None of them was exactly like the Rolls-Royce camouflage of his Space-Hopper. Most of them were a lot smaller, Gizzmo noticed, but that didn't matter. They were big enough to provide him with cover.

Keeping low, Gizzmo darted from one earth-vehicle to the next. As he got closer to the training camp, he risked a peek at what was happening.

Nothing. The parade ground was empty.

Why?

Of course, reasoned Gizzmo, the star thugs must be inside the building, learning more horrific acts of thuggery to practise on unsuspecting stars no doubt. What better time could there be for him to sneak in and find out what they were up to? If only he could avoid the guards. There are bound to be guards, thought Gizzmo.

He was nearly right. Creeping forward until he was almost opposite the front gate, Gizzmo saw to his surprise that, instead of the whole host of guards he'd expected, there was just one.

'Only one guard, BrainBox?' murmured Gizzmo.

The computer stayed silent.

'Just one? And he . . .' Gizzmo looked again, '. . . he looks like he's washing the training camp's sign-board! Funny. Very funny. What do you think, BrainBox?'

'Not thinking,' moaned BrainBox.

Gizzmo glanced down at the computer tucked beneath his arm. 'Not thinking. They're over-confident you mean? Haven't considered the possibility of a smart secret agent like me penetrating their defences? Yes, I do believe you're right, BrainBox. They're just not thinking.'

Gizzmo took another peek. 'Do you know what I think?'

'One doesn't even know what oneself thinks,' said BrainBox with a sigh.

'I think,' said Gizzmo, 'that I could run straight into that building without that guard seeing me.'

And the more he looked, the more sure he became. The guard was still hard at work behind the sign-board. Gizzmo could only see his legs, which meant, knowing what Gizzmo now knew about earth-creature's bodies, that the guard couldn't see him at all.

Yes, it could work!

'Ready, BrainBox?' he hissed. 'Here . . . goes!'

* * *

28

Oh dear, thought Dobson, the St Arthur's care-taker, what do I do now?

He paused, mid-mop, to consider the question more deeply.

Had he, or had he not, just seen a boy with a box under his arm scamper through the front gate and into the school building?

Yes, he had.

So, what should he do about it?

Hmmm.

What had Miss Hart's instructions been? 'If any of those grotty little herberts tries to get out of this school before going-home time, Dobson, wring their scrawny neck. Oh, and by the way Dobson – if any of the grotty little herberts *does* get out of this school before going-home time, I will wring *your* neck.'

Crystal clear. Dobson broke out in a sweat just thinking about it.

But what had Miss Hart said about stopping those who tried to get *in* to the school?'

Nothing.

The caretaker gave a nod of satisfaction. That's what he would do, then. Nothing.

He mopped his brow with relief, and went back to work.

Gizzmo dived through the peeling wooden doors and flattened himself against the wall. They'd made it! They were inside the star thugs' training camp!

He looked around. A dingy-grey corridor ran away to the left, a dingy-grey one to the right. In

29

front of him a third dingy-grey corridor stretched away into the distance. The whole place looked, thought Gizzmo, as grey and miserable as . . . well, as BrainBox had been looking ever since they'd landed.

He looked along the three corridors. Which way now?

Left, he decided, as the muffled sound of a voice drifted out from behind one of the doors along that dingy-grey corridor.

Keeping close to the wall, Gizzmo tiptoed up to it. Would he hear something useful? Something that would tell him whether these star thugs were as dangerous as they seemed?

'Space travel,' he heard the voice behind the door say, 'is one of the wonders of science . . .'

'Science, BrainBox,' whispered Gizzmo, 'it must be an instructor, telling the star thugs about Science.'

'. . . who can forget that wonderful night when the moon was conquered . . .'

'Moon? Conquered?'

'. . . and Neil Armstrong became a modern-day hero for thousands of would-be astronauts . . .'

Gizzmo stood up straight. 'Armstrong? Neil Armstrong? Does that name mean anything to you, BrainBox?'

The computer flickered on and off slowly.

'Arrrrmmmmstronngg. Armm. Strongg.'

It began to glow brighter and brighter, and speak faster and faster.

'Arm. Strong. Arm. Strong. Strong. Arm. Strong-arm. Strong-arm tactics, force, lots of force, beat 'em up, smash 'em in, sort 'em out, thuggery, thug, thug, thug . . .'

BrainBox slowed down for a moment, then started up again faster than ever.

'Kneel, kneel, kneel down, bend down, on your knees, on the ground, kneel armstrong, kneel strong-arm, beat 'em up on the ground, kick a man while he's down, dowwnn, dowwwnnn . . .'

BrainBox faded with a sigh, but he'd said enough for Gizzmo.

The star thugs were being taught about an earth-hero – a Neil Armstrong, a moon conqueror who was clearly none other than the first-ever star thug!

Gizzmo moved on down the corridor, to a door from behind which he could hear very different sounds.

Zapping, sizzling, exploding, screeching, blood-curdling sounds.

The door was slightly ajar. Gizzmo risked a look inside. The sight was horrific. Wild-eyed star thugs were sitting in front of screens, hitting buttons and screaming things like, 'Eat cosmic dust!' and 'Take that, alien!'

Suddenly the star thug nearest the door turned round.

Gizzmo tried to back away before he was seen. Too late. The star thug reached out and grabbed him by the collar.

'Computer club members only, scumbag!' the star thug snarled, before shoving Gizzmo out into the corridor and slamming the door.

'Computer club?' said Gizzmo.

BrainBox stirred again. 'Commmpuuuterrr.

31

Com-puuterr. Like oneself when one is feeling well, brainy, very useful, jolly clever . . .' Then, all in a rush, 'club, club together, club, truncheon, heavy stick, big stick, give 'em stick, bash 'em up, weapon, bash 'em up weaponnnnns . . .'

That's it, thought Gizzmo. If the star thugs were receiving computer-assisted alien-zapping weapons-training then the whole galaxy was in mortal danger.

He had to get back to the Space-Hopper and report the dreadful news to The General at once.

Turning away from the unnerving sounds of the star thugs' computerized clubbing, Gizzmo began to scurry back towards the way out.

He still hadn't reached the front door when the alarm bells started to ring.

Dobson the caretaker knew just what to do when the bell rang to signal the start of the lunch break.

Stop any of the grotty little herberts getting out, that was what.

He strode across to the front gates. There, crouching like a soldier with bayonet fixed, he jabbed the mop out in front of him.

Let them all come.

He'd wipe them out.

Gizzmo started running.

Somebody had raised the alarm! They were on to him!

Star thugs were pouring out of every door. They were coming for him!

32

He had to get out, fast!

Clutching BrainBox tightly, Gizzmo shot down the corridor and dived through the training camp's front door. He would go out the way he'd come in.

No he wouldn't! He couldn't. The guard was there at the gates, waiting for him and looking really fierce.

Then what could he do? What did the Sigma–6 Secret Service Handbook recommend at times like this? SSSSH page 29, paragraph 2 (c) came to him in a flash.

WHAT TO DO WHEN YOU'RE IN THE ENEMY CAMP, THE ALARM HAS GONE OFF, THEY'RE ALL AFTER YOU AND YOU CAN'T GO OUT THE FRONT WAY –

Go out the back way.

Of course! Out the back way! There was always a back way!

Gizzmo skidded sharp left, along the front of the building and sharp left again.

He followed the building as far as he could, then went sharp left again.

Yes, there it was!

The back way!

It was right in front of him!

All he had to do was hurtle through it, and he'd be free and heading for the safety of his Space-Hopper.

Gizzmo hurtled.

Strangely, he immediately discovered that he

wasn't free. Quite the opposite in fact. He was very unfree. A large and imposing guard with grey frizzy hair on its head and a very unpleasant look on its face had leapt out from the shadows and grabbed him.

A large and imposing guard who caused Gizzmo's heart to sink as she said, 'And where do you think you're going, you grotty little herbert?'

5

Parking Problems

Lionel A. Fothergill's heart, unlike Gizzmo's, was thumping in excitement.

Not that Lionel A. Fothergill was the sort that usually got excited. He was not. In his days as a pupil at St Arthur's High School – days which had ended some two years previously – he had been known as LAF-a-minute for the very reason that he seemed to get excited about absolutely nothing at all.

Lionel A. Fothergill had had the last LAF, however. His success in landing a job with the District Council had been in no small part due to his total lack of excitability. The District Council didn't want excitable persons in the particular line of work for which they'd chosen Lionel.

No, no. It was not to excitable persons that the Council entrusted:

– one uniform, black (for the wearing of);
– one cap, black with yellow band (for the wearing of), said yellow band clearly marked with the words 'Traffic Warden';
– one pair of boots, black (for the wearing out of);
– one pencil, (for the writing with);

– one pad of parking tickets (for the filling in of, with plenty more where they came from).

No indeed, Lionel had been entrusted with these valuable items of Council property for the purposes of keeping, in a very unexcitable manner, the district's streets and car parks free of unwanted vehicles.

And yet, at this very moment, Lionel A. Fothergill – try as he might – just couldn't stop himself from feeling really, really excited.

For the vehicle he was staring at right now, up here on the very top storey of the multi-storey car park, was quite the most excitingly unwanted vehicle he had seen in the whole of his short traffic-wardening career.

Lionel stroked his trainee moustache, a scraggy thin black line above his top lip, like the tidemark from a liquorice milkshake.

Perhaps he should check once more, just to be sure.

Slowly he walked around the offending vehicle, looking for the sticky whatsit the Council required to be stuck inside one of its windows to show that it was authorized for parking in a car park authorized for such parking.

Lionel's heart leapt for joy. No sign of any sticky whatsit at all!

He flicked open his pad of parking tickets. He licked the end of his pencil. He began to write. He stopped.

Was there something else about this particular vehicle he had noticed? Or, rather, something he had not noticed?

There was.

The vehicle had no tax disc. No number plate, either.

Lionel's heart cancelled the leaping for joy bit and turned a double-somersault instead. No sticky whatsit, no tax disc, no number plate!

His mum was going to be so proud of him!

He, Lionel A. Fothergill, had found, for the first time ever, a car that met all the requirements for being towed away!

And it was a Rolls-Royce as well!

6

A Table For Two

Captured! By the Enemy! Oh, the shame of it!

Gizzmo stood before the large, frizzy-haired guard and resolved to divulge nothing but his name, rank and serial number even if she shone a bright light in his eyes to torch-ure him mercilessly.

For her part, Stony was feeling a little ashamed herself.

Try as she might, she couldn't actually put a name to the face of the pupil she'd just nabbed.

In fact, she couldn't say with any honesty that she actually recognized him at all. This was awkward. If the grotty little herbert realized she didn't know who he was then her reputation as a headmistress who knew who was who and what was what could be severely dented.

She would have to play this one carefully.

'I said, where do you think you're going?'

Gizzmo said nothing. The guard spoke again.

'Nobody leaves this establishment without my permission. Do you understand that?'

Permission? Gizzmo gave a quick glance upwards. If this person gave permission for star thugs to go on leave then she was much more than a simple guard.

There was only one explanation.

He'd been captured by the star thugs' commanding officer!

'Try to leave this establishment without permission and you will land yourself in hot water! Got that?'

Still Gizzmo said nothing.

From beneath his arm, though, there came a high-pitched squeak. 'Hottt waatter,' said Brain-Box, 'hot water, hot water, old boiler . . .'

'What!' roared the star thugs' commanding officer.

She's getting angry, thought Gizzmo. He shook Brainbox hard, but this only seemed to make the computer squeak on even more. 'Boil, boil, boil-in-the-bag, old bag . . .'

'How dare you!'

' . . . bag, boil-in-the-bag, boil, poach, grill, fry, cook, cooker, hot, very hot, good for cooking, cook food, food, get some foooooood insssidde meee . . .'

Stony stared open-mouthed. Whatever next? First it was fashion holdalls. Then backpacks with TV characters splattered all over them.

And now . . . she looked at the box under the grotty little herbert's arm and shook her head in despair . . . talking lunch-boxes!

Given that she still couldn't recall the name of the pupil in her grasp there was, she decided, only one thing to do. Let him go.

'We do not take our lunch for a walk,' she said in

her most patient voice as she released her grip, 'we take it into the dining hall. Over there.'

Stony sighed. The grotty little herbert hadn't moved. Obviously a St Arthur's pupil – look dumb and act dumber.

'Well?' she said. 'Go on. What are you waiting for? Are you backward, boy?'

And with that she turned on her heel and stomped off.

Gizzmo was confused. What had he been told to do? Where had he been told to go?

Had he been captured or hadn't he?

'What's happening BrainBox?' he whispered.

The computer flickered half-heartedly. 'Backward boy. Yob. Nasty person. Thug.'

Thug! So that was it.

The transformation tablet had worked better than anybody could have hoped. Even the star thugs' commanding officer had been fooled. She'd mistaken him for a star thug. He was inside their camp, and with permission! Brilliant!

With renewed confidence, Gizzmo made his way towards the building he'd been shown. To the dining hall, whatever that was.

It was a place where there was a lot more din than din-dins.

Ros and Masher had arrived there some minutes earlier to find the place in its usual state of uproar. Bits of food were flying through the air, along with plastic beakers, knives, forks and the occasional dinner lady. What was more, every table, every chair, was occupied.

Masher looked around. 'Where d'you wanna sit, Ros?' said Masher.

'My usual, I think,' said Ros, pointing to a crowded table in the middle of the chaos, 'over there.'

'Right you are,' said Masher.

He elbowed his way across the hall. By the time he'd dusted a chair off with the sleeve of his blazer, and the spindly first-former he'd dusted off had picked himself up and hobbled away, the table had miraculously become free.

Ros sat down with a sigh. 'A UFO,' she said, 'a real-live UFO. And we saw it come down.'

'We did, didn't we?' said Masher, pulling up a chair for himself.

'And what can we do about it?' asked Ros.

'Dunno,' said Masher. 'What can we do about it?'

'Nothing! If we don't turn up for Maths, Stony will . . .'

'Have our guts for starters?' asked Masher.

'Right,' said Ros with a scowl. Life was so unfair.

Masher frowned. He didn't like to see Ros unhappy. 'Look on the bright side,' he said.

'What?'

'No lessons for a while,' said Masher. 'It's lunchtime.' He got to his feet and surveyed the dining hall. 'So, whose lunch do you fancy then?'

'What a noise!' moaned BrainBox.

Gizmo couldn't help but agree. The noise had grown with every step they'd taken towards the star thugs' dining hall place.

41

But now they were there, and actually standing outside the door, it was deafening. Gizzmo peeped inside and immediately saw why.

The sight was incredible. The hall was filled with rows and rows of tables, at which sat rows and rows of star thugs. All having rows by the look of them.

'Golly,' breathed Gizzmo. If they were like this to each other, what were they capable of doing to a nice friendly planet like Sigma–6?

And the noise! BrainBox was groaning again.

'It's no good,' said the computer. 'I can't stand it. I'm going to close down for a while.'

'Close down? What do you mean, close down?'

'Turn off and turn in. Have a sleep. The rest might do me some good.'

'But you can't!' hissed Gizzmo.

'I can,' said BrainBox, 'and I am. Goooooddnighhht.'

And with a final gurgle the computer's colour drained away to nothingness.

Now what? thought Gizzmo. He'd been banking on BrainBox having a few bright ideas on what to do next.

He took another peek into the dining hall. It still looked a terrible sight but, in the middle of it all, he noticed, one table was fairly calm.

There were just two star thugs sitting at it, one a slim girl-type, the other a bulky boy-type, and all the other star thugs seemed to be staying well clear of them.

No they weren't, realized Gizzmo. Not completely.

The boy-type was calling smaller star thugs to him. They came to the table, left some food, and went away again.

What did it mean? It meant they were senior star thugs, of course. And, as senior star thugs, they probably knew more about what was going on than most of the others. So, if he could eavesdrop on what they were saying it might give him even more valuable information to report back to The General.

Gizzmo inched his way inside the hall doors. What he needed to do was get closer to the two senior star thugs. But how? He shifted the silent BrainBox to his other arm while he thought about the problem.

'I'm still peckish, Masher,' said Ros. She looked down at the collection of empty lunch-boxes in front of her. 'Mothers don't seem to be providing substantial enough food for their children nowadays,' she said. 'It just isn't good enough.'

'Say no more,' said Masher. 'You want some afters, right?'

'Dessert,' said Ros. 'In refined circles, it's called dessert.'

'Yeh?' said Masher, who thought a refined circle was where the bloke with the whistle stood when a football match kicked off. 'Dessert it is, then.'

Masher lumbered to his feet and gazed round the dining hall again. Being a bread winner – not to mention a crisp winner, apple winner, chocolate bar winner and winner of everything else that was necessary to see that his beloved Ros received a nourishing and well-balanced diet – was getting tougher every day.

He'd already persuaded most of the regulars to contribute to the cause. Who was there left? Masher scratched his head. What he really needed – yeh, why hadn't he thought of it before? – what he really needed was to find somebody . . . new. Somebody with . . . a big . . . lunch-box.

Somebody like . . . him, over there.

Rolling his sleeves up to his elbows, Masher rumbled across the dining hall floor.

Well! thought Gizzmo. What a stroke of luck!

There he'd been, wondering how he could get close to the two important star thugs, when the boy-type had come over and actually invited *him* to join *them*!

Quite why the boy-type had twisted his arm up behind his left ear, Gizzmo wasn't too sure. An earth-custom, perhaps.

Anyway, here he was. What could he find out?

'Welcome,' the girl-type was saying.

'Thanks very much,' said Gizzmo.

'New here are you?'

Gizzmo nodded. 'Yes. Very.'

'Thought so. Well that being the case you qualify for a special introductory offer.' The girl-type smiled at him as she spoke. He was fooling them!

Act dumb, thought Gizzmo. Let them do the talking. 'I do?' he said.

'Yep,' said the boy-type, with an unnecessarily firm repeat of the arm-twist-behind-the-ear custom, 'you do.'

The girl-type smiled again. 'It works like this,'

she said, 'My name is Ros. This is Masher. That's the introductory bit. Now you have to offer us what you've got in that box of yours.'

Gizzmo realized what was happening too late. Before he knew it, the Masher-thug had let go of his arm and snatched BrainBox from his grip.

'No!' yelled Gizzmo.

'Yes!' shouted Masher.

'You can't!'

'We have,' purred Ros.

Gizzmo couldn't understand it. They'd been so friendly. 'Give it back!' he yelled. 'It's not mine!'

'Not now it ain't!' guffawed Masher. 'It belongs to Ros. She wants a dessert!'

Desert? The Ros-thug wanted to desert? Run away, did she mean?

Gizzmo was caught in two minds.

Should he own up about who he was and where he'd come from and say he'd be only too happy to help them escape?

Or should he risk his life by leaping at the Masher-thug and trying to get BrainBox back?

All things considered, then, there couldn't have been a worse time for the transformation tablet to start wearing off.

7

Problems, Problems

As he felt his body starting to change back into its Sigma–6 shape, Gizzmo knew that desperate measures were called for.

If he didn't do something quickly his secret would be out. He wouldn't be a secret agent any more. Not even a fairly secret agent. He'd be a well - it's - certainly - no - secret - where - you - come - from-is-it-agent.

So he did something quickly.

He shot out of the dining hall, down the corridor and through the first door he came to.

It was a door marked 'Boys'.

Masher watched Gizzmo go. 'He didn't look too bright, did he?'

'Takes one to know one,' said Ros.

'Uh?'

Ros waved a hand. 'Forget it, Mastermind. What's in his box?'

Masher put one brawny arm round BrainBox and tugged at the computer's lid. He tugged again. 'Dunno,' he said. 'I can't open it.'

'Try harder.'

'I am trying, Ros,' said Masher.

'You can say that again,' said Ros.

As the school bell rang to signal the end of the lunch break, Ros stood up with a theatrical sigh. 'Come on, then. Let's go. Stony'll be looking out for us.'

Masher stopped tugging and lifted up Brain-Box. 'What shall I do with this, Ros?'

'What do you think, thicko? If it's locked it means the new kid must have put something worth having inside. Bring it with you, of course.'

'Right,' said Masher. He frowned as what Ros had said to him sunk in slowly, like a stray marble sinking into a vat of school custard. 'And I ain't a thicko, Ros.'

'No?' said Ros loftily.

'No,' said Masher, tucking the new kid's lunch-box under his arm. 'I got a brain you know.'

Behind the door marked 'Boys', Gizzmo was congratulating himself on managing to find such a perfect place in his hour of need.

Not only had he found a room that was empty, he'd even found one with a row of little cubicles to hide in! He picked the nearest one and slammed the door shut.

He wasn't a moment too soon.

Almost at once his schoolboy body went pee-onnggg, scrrm-mmph, gdd-onnggg and he found himself back in his old, familiar Sigma—6 shape again.

Now what?

He had to get BrainBox back, he knew that much. Going home and telling The General that he'd lost a super-brain on his first job was some-

47

thing that Gizzmo didn't fancy at all. He'd rather not go back.

In fact, now he thought about it, he *couldn't* go back – not without BrainBox. The computer was the one who knew the way home.

Yes, he had to get BrainBox back. But how?

Gizzmo sat down on the cubicle's little seat and began to think.

A fair bit of thinking was going on further down the corridor as well.

Ros was thinking that whoever invented maths, and more especially maths teachers, should have been drowned at birth.

After looking at the box on Ros's desk and thinking that he must be losing his strength if he couldn't open a simple little thing like that, Masher had turned to thinking that Ros looked really ace when she was thinking.

And, at the front of the class, Stony Hart was thinking that never, in all her years in teaching, had she met a thicker class than the one sitting before her at that very moment.

'Page 23, Miscellaneous Exercises,' she announced.

Pages were turned, flipped, scrunched or ripped out for easy reference.

'Number 1,' continued Stony. 'A man buys 2 cans of lager and 1 bottle of wine for £5. Another man buys 2 bottles of wine and 1 can of lager for £7. How much does a bottle of wine cost, and how much does a can of lager cost?'

Stony glared at the two pupils over in the far

corner of the room, kept apart from the rest of the class for their safety – for the rest of the class's safety, that was.

'Miss Price?'

Ros scowled. 'Dunno, Miss.'

'You were supposed to do this for homework last night.'

'My Dad wouldn't let me, Miss. He says I mustn't have anything to do with drink.'

Stony turned to Masher. 'McTurk. Any idea?'

Masher shrugged. 'A week?'

'What!'

'A week?' repeated Masher.

Stony closed her eyes in despair. 'How can a bottle of wine cost a week, for heaven's sake!'

'Ask my old man,' said Masher. 'Wine's weak,' he says, 'give me a bottle of scotch any day.'

The class laughed, then unlaughed as Stony glared around. 'Has anybody done this question?' she growled.

Nobody put their hand up.

'Then do it now!' She marched to the classroom door.

'And by the time I come back you'd better have some answers for me! Or there'll be trouble.'

As the sound of Stony's voice reverberated down the corridor, Gizzmo almost froze to the seat he was sitting on.

It wasn't so much the sound of that voice, awful as it was. It was what it had said.

'By the time I come back you'd better have some

49

answers for me!' the star thugs' commanding officer had said.

'Or there'll be trouble!' she'd said.

Gizzmo groaned. This was terrible. The Ros-thug and the Masher-thug must have changed their minds about deserting and taken BrainBox straight to their leader.

'By the time I come back you'd better have some answers for me!' that's what he'd just heard her say.

It was obvious what was happening. BrainBox was being interrogated!

Clearly the computer was being brave, though. The star thugs' leader hadn't got any answers yet. That was why she was so mad. But how long could BrainBox hold out? What if the computer cracked under the strain and spilled the greens? What would it tell them?

There was only one course open to him, Gizzmo decided. He was going to have to get into that room and find out what was being said.

Another transformation tablet was called for.

But he didn't want to look like a star thug this time. He had to become something different. Something that wouldn't be noticed. Something small.

Gizzmo opened the box of transformation tablets and began to sort through them.

In the classroom, Ros and Masher were no nearer to sorting out their problem.

'This question is ridiculous,' moaned Ros. 'A decent bottle of Beaujolais would cost more than a fiver. How the geezer in this question can get

50

two cans of lager at the same time is beyond me.'

'The whole question's beyond me,' said Masher.

'And anyway, we shouldn't be here.'

'We should. It's definitely maths. We have it this time every week.'

'I mean, knucklehead, we should be out there looking for that UFO. And we would have been, but for U-know-who.' Ros returned to doodling in her maths book, jabbing her pencil angrily into a sketch of Stony.

Masher returned to chewing the end of his pencil and wondering why nobody had ever come up with strawberry-flavoured pencils instead of wood-flavoured ones.

Which is why, engrossed as they were, neither of them noticed BrainBox slowly flicker back to life.

The computer was feeling a lot better. Not perfect, but a lot better than before.

How perfect though? That was the question.

BrainBox quickly ran some self-tests on its neural network and memory banks.

Memories of leaving Sigma–6: COMPLETE
Memories of journey: COMPLETE
Memories of landing: PAINFUL, but
COMPLETE
Memories of what Gizzmo Lewis looked like
after taking transformation tablet: VAGUE
Memories of what had happened between then
and now: MISSING

Could be worse, decided BrainBox. Just one small lapse of memory. And any self-respecting mega-brain should be able to fill in the missing bit. It was a simple process of deduction, surely.

What were the available facts?

1) Last known memory: one was in the possession of Gizzmo Lewis, secret agent, busy transforming himself into a boy earth-creature.

2) Present known position: one was in the possession of one boy earth-creature and one girl earth-creature.

Conclusion. Easy, concluded BrainBox. The boy must be the transformed Gizzmo Lewis, and the girl a real earth-creature that he has made contact with in an attempt to find out whether earth-creatures are friendly or not.

And not making much progress by the sound of it, thought BrainBox, as his aural receivers picked up their voices.

'I mean . . .' it was the earth-girl talking, '. . . what use is algebra? None at all.'

'Oh, I dunno. They look nice. All stripey, and that.'

'Algebra! Not Zebra! Bonehead.'

No, Lewis was not making much progress at all. If the earth-girl was going to be impressed by a superior Sigma intelligence then there was only one place it was going to come from.

One, decided BrainBox, was going to have to speak up.

'If you ask me,' said Ros, 'the person who invented algebra should be shot.'

'Not logical.'

'Pardon?' said Ros, her voice as cold as a polar bear's nose. Ros was not used to being argued with.

'I didn't say nuffink,' said Masher.

'Assertion that person who invented algebra should be shot, not logical,' repeated the voice. 'Earth-algebra was invented in earth-year 350. Earth-guns were not invented until earth-year 1326. Therefore, the inventor of algebra could not have been shot.'

Ros looked at Masher.

Masher looked back at Ros, his mouth even more open than usual.

They both looked round.

The voice hadn't come from anybody else in the class. Nobody was sitting close enough to them to have spoken that clearly.

Then they noticed BrainBox, now glowing a healthy pink on Ros's desk.

'It . . . it . . . that . . . it . . . c-came from that,' stammered Ros.

'Said it weren't me, didn't I?' said Masher.

Ros was too amazed to insult him. 'F-from that,' she said again. 'It . . . spoke. That kid's lunch-box *spoke*!'

BrainBox was seriously offended.

'Do you mind? Lunch-box, indeed. One will have you know that you are talking to none other than BrainBox, the finest mind to be found on the planet Sigma–6, if not the whole of the Xelphon constellation.

'And to prove it, the answer to that pathetically easy question you are struggling with is . . .'

8
Going Up The Wall

Back in the security of his little cubicle, Gizzmo was still sifting through his box of transformation tablets.

Something small, that's what he wanted to become.

He thought hard. Could he remember – did SSSSH have any advice on the subject?

SURVEILLANCE
When it comes to surveillance, good secret agents are as unobtrusive as a fly on a wall. That's the way they get the buzz about what's going on.

Hmmm. Could he turn himself into a wall? Hardly.

A fly, then? Yes, of course! A fly! Every planet in the universe had flies. Sigma–6 certainly did: nasty, whizzy little things that ruined your picnic by trying to nick what you'd picked.

A fly on the wall. That was it!

Hurriedly, Gizzmo searched through the box of transformation tablets looking for one marked 'fly'.

Nothing.

He checked again.

Nothing again. Not a single 'fly' tablet in the whole collection.

He tried one last time.

Aha!

Gizzmo plucked a yellow transformation tablet from the collection. He read what was marked on it.

'Flea'.

Not exactly what he was after, but there couldn't be that much difference between an earth-fly and an earth-flea could there?

Carefully he placed the box of transformation tablets on the floor. With the cubicle's door locked they would be safe enough.

The yellow transformation tablet he swallowed with a gulp.

Once again he felt the peculiar sensation of his normal Sigma–6 body changing shape. This time he was being squeezed and squashed and flattened, as though he was being run over by one of the Moonistry of the Environmoont's heaviest scream-rollers.

Then he was shrinking, shrinking, shrinking . . .

The feelings stopped. Gizzmo looked at himself. Brilliant! He now had a tiny round body and a set of very skinny legs. But, most of all, he was small! Now he could sneak in anywhere without being noticed.

He flapped various bits. Funny. He didn't seem able to fly. Maybe that was how earth-flies and earth-fleas were different. He tried again.

B-doiingg!

Great Galactic Sky-Skippers! I might not be

able to fly, thought Gizzmo, but I can certainly jump!

Taking care not to over-use his brilliant new jumping powers, Gizzmo hopped under the locked cubicle door, across the floor and out through the door leading into the corridor.

He wasn't a moment too soon. Up ahead, the star thugs' commanding officer was just returning to the interrogation room.

B-doingg! B-doingg! B-doingg!!!

I'm coming BrainBox! Be strong! Don't tell them anything!

Gizzmo Lewis is springing to the rescue!

Ros hardly noticed as Stony marched back into the classroom. Her mind was still spinning with what BrainBox had said.

This thing, this box on her desk, was claiming to be a super-computer from another planet.

Could it be true? If it was, could it also mean that what they'd seen come down on top of the multi-storey really had been a UFO? And that the new kid who'd belted off before Masher belted him was an alien?

The possibilities were mind-boggling. All this news, waiting to be told – better still, sold – to the world by the one person who knew about it.

Her.

Famous, thought Ros, I'll be famous. The opportunities were endless. Pictures in the newspapers, TV interviews, chat shows, guest appearances – she would be a star; a starlet at the very least.

But only if it was all true.

She looked BrainBox in the vision sensor. 'Tell me,' she began, 'that new kid . . .'

Stony's bellow stopped her finishing the question. 'A bottle of wine and two cans of lager for £5. Two bottles of wine and a can of lager for £7. How much for a bottle, how much for a can? Right, who's got an answer?'

Ros looked again at the box on her desk. A super-brain, eh? There was one way to find out. Slowly, she put her hand up.

'Well, well. Miss Price. This should be interesting.'

'A bottle of wine costs . . .' Ros quickly checked the numbers BrainBox had rattled off earlier, '£3 and a can of lager £1.'

'Nonsense,' snorted Stony. 'That is quite wrong. Quite, quite . . . er . . . oh . . . quite . . . right.' The teacher blinked. She checked the answers at the back of her book again. 'Yes,' she said in a stunned voice, 'quite right.'

Her eyes narrowed. This was suspicious. Girls like Rosalind Price did not put their hands up in maths lessons and answer difficult questions. Even less did they get the answers right.

'Your ability in this subject appears to have increased dramatically Miss Price,' said Stony. 'Over the last ten minutes, in fact. Shall we give this wonderful new prowess a further test. By asking you to do number 14, perhaps?'

Ros gulped. She looked down at her maths book. Question 14 was so full of squiggles and funny numbers it looked like the sort of soup her mum used to dish up when she was younger. She couldn't understand any of it. This really would be a test for a super-brain.

Bending low as if she was working something out, Ros slid the page in front of BrainBox's vision sensors.

'Come on then clever-dick,' she whispered, 'if you're what you say you are, what's the answer to number 14?'

'Boring,' said BrainBox instantly, 'X is 4 point 1 and Y is the square root of 6.'

'Er . . . is . . . er . . . X equal to 4 point 1,' repeated Ros, 'and . . . er . . . Y the square root of 6?'

'Ye-es,' said Stony slowly. 'Right again.'

Her suspicions deepened.

Rosalind Price, mathematical genius? No.

Rosalind Price, excuse genius, with 1001 ready-made reasons for being late in the morning, yes. But mathematical genius? Definitely, absolutely, not.

Something, thought Stony, is going on here. Something, perhaps, to do with that talking lunch-box on the girl's desk?

Something that she should investigate, of that she was sure.

Grim-faced, Stony marched towards the back of the classroom.

Ros saw Stony approaching.

Panic set in. If the old battle-axe discovered BrainBox everything would be ruined. All her big, star-studded, money-making dreams would be shattered.

She had to get up to the top of the multi-storey car park and find that UFO.

She had to get out.

But how?

It would take a pretty big computer to solve *this* problem.

She was wrong on both counts. Her solution didn't come from a computer.

Nor was it very big.

Her solution was actually very small and, though she didn't know it, had just hopped through the classroom door and started climbing up the wall.

Even though things looked pretty different when you were on your side and half-way up a wall, Gizzmo could see that his worst fears had been confirmed.

BrainBox *was* being interrogated – and, by the looks of it, not only by the star thugs' commanding officer but by the Ros-thug, the Masher-thug and a whole room full of trainee interrogators!

Gizzmo b-ddoingged along the wall a bit further. Even though the situation was bad, he couldn't help feeling pretty pleased with himself and his new flea shape.

What a brilliant disguise! He'd hear everything that was being said.

He wasn't wrong. At that moment something was said, and Gizzmo heard it very clearly.

'Please Miss Hart,' somebody said, 'there's a flea on the wall.'

Ros couldn't believe her luck. There she'd been, wondering how to hop it, and the answer was in front of her, hopping itself.

'A flea!' she screamed. 'It's a flea!'

Everybody swivelled round to look.

'A great big enormous flea!'

Masher started to say, 'It's only a little one, Ros, nuffink to worry ab . . . ow!' before being stopped by a sharp poke in the ribs from Ros's compass.

Ros was on her feet now, waving her arms about and looking panic-stricken. 'Fleas! I'm allergic to fleas!'

'Calm down, Miss Price,' said Stony.

But Ros had no intention of calming down. 'Let me out!' she yelled. 'I've got to get out! Everybody out!'

The rest of the class didn't need telling twice. Whether or not Ros was really scared they didn't know, but a command of 'everybody out' was too good to miss.

Chairs and desks went flying as they all dived for the door.

Ros pulled Masher out of his seat by the hair. 'Grab that,' she yelled, pointing at BrainBox.

Masher couldn't see what all the fuss was about, but he did what he was told and snatched up the computer.

'Now what?' he said, following Ros as she

elbowed her way through the scrum of excited bodies.

'We're off, that's what!' yelled Ros.

'Where?'

'UFO-hunting, of course! C'mon!'

They raced out of the building. Fame, Ros was thinking, there's nothing standing between me and fame!

Well, next to nothing. Dobson was back on guard at the front gate with his mop and bucket.

'Halt!' demanded the caretaker. 'Friend or foe?'

'Foe,' said Ros. 'Deal with him Masher.'

'At once, Ros.'

A moment later, a perfectly-aimed conker sent the mop spinning from Dobson's hand.

And, moments after that, the caretaker found himself dangling from the St Arthur's sign-board by the collar of his brown coat.

'Well done Masher,' said Ros crisply, already on the move again. 'Bye, Dobson! Keep your chin up!'

'Come back!' Stony had screamed as pupils flew past her on all sides. It had been a waste of breath.

The classroom, *her* classroom, had become all room and no class. And why? She glared at the wall. All because of that thing.

With a cold look in her eye, Stony picked up her heavy maths book.

On the wall, Gizzmo was feeling confused.

Why had all the star thugs started screaming

and charging about as though they were scared stiff? He didn't know.

Was an earth-flea capable of doing something nasty to an earth-creature? Gizzmo was itching to find out. Maybe he should recommend to The General that they invade the Earth looking like fleas?

The thought crossed his mind . . . and then went straight out the other side, as he realized to his horror that becoming an earth-flea had one very big drawback to it.

The drawback that, when you became one, you were just the right size for an earth-creature to draw back her arm and flatten you with a maths book!

B-doinngg! went Gizzmo.

Splatt! went Stony's book on the wall.

Gizzmo felt the wind whistle past where his ear would have been if he'd had one. The book started to come at him again.

He jumped again.

B-doinngg! Splatt!

And again.

B-doinngg! Splatt!

And again, and again, and again.

B-doinngg! Splatt! B-doinngg! Splatt! B-doinngg! Splatt!

Gizzmo was gasping for breath. His legs were tiring. The splatts! were getting closer.

He knew what he had to do. The flea had to flee. But where to? He needed somewhere dark. Somewhere out of sight.

He looked around desperately.

The star thugs' commanding officer was coming at him again. She was raising the book above her head again.

It was at that instant that Gizzmo saw the chance of an escape route. Somewhere dark. Somewhere out of sight.

Bbb-dddoooiiiinggggg!!!

With one mighty leap, Gizzmo sprang away from the wall and straight down the front of Stony's blouse.

9

When You've Got To Tow, You've Got To Tow

'Well done, Lionel!'

'Terrific!'

'This'll make their eyes pop down at the compound!'

'Long time since they've had one of these . . .'

'First one ever, I'd say . . .'

'You could get a promotion out of this, Lionel. Traffic warden, grade 2 at the very least . . .'

'I mean, anyone who books a Rolls-Royce has got to be a bit special . . .'

'But to get one towed away . . .'

'Magic.'

Lionel A. Fothergill smiled happily, his little moustache doing a twitchy dance above his top lip.

'Thanks Gladys,' he said to the driver – correction, Vehicle Removals Operative – as she leapt up into the cab of her vehicle removals vehicle.

'Any time, Lionel,' said Gladys. She sucked hard on her pipe as she fired the lorry into life. It gave off a cloud of thick black smoke. So did the lorry.

A little tear of joy trickled down Lionel's cheek as he watched his first-ever Rolls-Royce being towed away from the top floor of the multi-storey car park.

Oh, his mum was going to be so proud of him!

10
Gizzmo In The Dark

'Aaaaagggh!' screamed Stony, 'Eeeeekkk! Oooooohhh!!'

She thumped herself wildly as the tickling began inside her vest.

This was no laughing matter.

Gizzmo didn't think it was funny either.

It had been dangerous on the wall, but this was even worse.

All around him bits of woolly stuff were being pounded, bouncing him up and down. It was worse than travelling on the Sigma underground in the crush hour.

It was no good. He had to get out. Gizzmo began to move. Maybe there's another exit, he thought.

He moved downwards in short little hops. Outside, the star thugs' commanding officer was still yelling. Inside, she was wriggling so madly he was having trouble keeping his footing. He slithered a bit further.

Suddenly he found himself up against an obstruction. He bounded to one side and tried again. No good. He jumped a bit further. A bit more. Still no good. The obstruction was too solid.

He was going to have to go back out the way he'd come in.

Beaten by Stony's extra-strong knicker elastic, Gizzmo started climbing.

As the tickling continued, Stony was in an agony of indecision.

The educational system was a failure, she realized that now. She'd been to teacher-training college, she'd had in-service training, she'd been on umpteen courses – and had she ever been offered advice on how to deal with a flea inside her blouse? Never.

What should she do? Carry on thumping and try to squash the ghastly thing? Take all her clothes off and let it hop away? What?

The decision was made for her. Gizzmo's attempts to find a way past Stony's knicker elastic had taken him some way from the route of his original descent. The result being that, when he started to climb again, it was up Stony's backbone.

As she felt the tickling between her shoulder blades, Stony realized that pummelling was out. She couldn't reach the flaming flea now. Stripping off was the only possible remedy.

But where? She couldn't do it where she was. Even in their greatest hours of need, head-mistresses did not strip down to their birthday suits in the middle of classrooms. No, she had to go somewhere out of sight.

Snatching up her handbag, Stony charged out of the now empty classroom, into the corridor, and through the first suitable door she came to.

It was a door marked 'Boys'.

Gizzmo was still climbing, but the going wasn't easy. The star thugs' commanding officer seemed to have stopped pummelling and started running instead. Being bounced up and down made it so difficult to get a foothold.

Gizzmo struggled on. How much further? He looked up. Light! He could see light!

Suddenly he heard a crash and the bouncing stopped. Gizzmo seized his chance.

With a couple of giant hops, he forced his way out from the back of Stony's collar and up into the concealing frizziness of her hair.

Throwing her handbag onto the floor, Stony ripped off her cardigan. She started to tear open the buttons of her blouse.

Then, as she felt Gizzmo's giant leap out from her collar she slapped the back of her neck. She looked at her hand. Nothing.

But, mercy of mercies, the thing seemed to have gone. She certainly couldn't feel the ghastly mixture of tickling and pinpricks any more.

She looked around the floor. The thing wasn't anywhere to be seen. Still, she thought with relief, it had gone. With a bit of luck, it would hop to the playground and end its days under a pair of strictly forbidden but extremely heavy Doc Martens.

As her jangling nerves began to settle, Stony noticed a bit more about her surroundings. She saw that, in her panic, she had not only galloped into the boys' toilets but had also smashed her way into a cubicle that, curiously, had been both locked and empty.

She also saw that when she'd thrown her handbag on the floor it had sprung open and scattered its contents all over the show. Muttering angrily to herself, Stony knelt down and began to pick them up again.

Comb, compact, pocket diary . . .

'Rosalind Price,' she muttered. 'She started it.'

. . . mirror, after-shave, pencil . . .

'Screaming her head off. Causing a panic. I bet she did it on purpose. Yes, of course she did! To cause a diversion!'

. . . nail-clippers, tweezers, thumbscrew . . .

Stony's blood began to boil. 'I bet she's on her way to the shopping centre now! Her and that cretin McTurk! Runaways, the pair of them!'

. . . sugar lumps, aspirins, box of transformation tablets . . .

In her rage, Stony scooped the remaining bits and pieces into her handbag without looking and jumped up.

'Right, you two!' she bellowed to the world at large, 'I'm coming after you!'

Hidden in the dense overgrowth on top of Stony's head, Gizzmo was considering his position. It wasn't good, but it could be worse.

The star thugs' commanding officer had got his transformation tablets. He'd seen her put them in her kit-bag. But at least he knew where they were.

And he also knew now that the Ros-thug and

the Masher-thug *were* deserters. What he must have seen was not just BrainBox under interrogation, but them as well. And now their commanding officer was out to bring them back.

So, reasoned Gizzmo, if he stayed where he was she would lead him to them.

Yes, there was no point in moving.

Hair he was, and hair he was going to stay.

11

Stony Gives Chase

At that precise moment, Gizzmo's computer was doing some haring of its own -- haring along the road to be exact. Apart from the kerfuffle with the earth-creature carrying a mop and bucket, they'd been running non-stop since they left.

BrainBox was not enjoying the experience.

'Oy!' the computer squawked as, firmly held under Masher's arm, it was bounced along a route which its memory circuits told it was the way they'd come before, only backwards, 'stop shaking me about! You know I'm delicate! You know I get headaches.'

'So do I,' puffed Masher. 'Maths gives me a headache. And geography. And English, and science and . . .'

Up ahead Ros had decided that a brief stop was called for. Spending her life sitting on walls munching other people's crisps meant that she was not as fit as she might be. A breather was called for and, anyway, there were some burning questions she needed to ask. Reaching a small alleyway, she took a sharp left turn and ducked inside.

Masher followed her in. Underneath his arm, BrainBox was still complaining.

'Headaches. Serious headaches. You know I suffer from them, Lewis. I shall report you to The

General when we get back. Mistreatment of a computer. That's a serious offence, that is.'

'What's it on about?' panted Ros, her breath slowly returning.

'Dunno,' shrugged Masher.

'You say you come from another planet?' said Ros.

'Planet Sigma–6 in the constellation of Xelphon,' replied BrainBox, 'as one told you earlier.'

'Far away is it?'

'Forty-three point two-seven-six light-years.'

'You don't say?' At the speed of light that was . . . that was a long way, decided Ros. 'Take a long time to get here did it?'

'Including an unscheduled stop in a lay-fly near Ursa Major because my friend here can't read a galaxy map . . .' BrainBox flickered angrily in the direction of Masher, 'about eighty-one tardons.'

'Eighty-one tardons?' said Ros. 'How long's that?'

'In your earth time,' said BrainBox, 'about three hours. The Mark 2 Whereami Orbital Outing Space-Hopper has a Hyper-Hop facility fitted as standard. A wonderful invention. I should know, I invented it. Didn't I, Lewis?' The computer flickered again in Masher's direction.

Masher frowned. Can't read a galaxy map? Hyper-Hop? What's it on about? 'What's it on about, Ros?' he said.

'Come on Lewis,' said BrainBox, 'thanks to me you've escaped. You can stop all this silly under-cover stuff now.'

Masher's frown frowned. 'Uhh?'

BrainBox lost patience. 'Oh, for goodness sake,

71

Lewis! You may look like a disgusting earth-creature, but you don't have to act like one!'

Masher's frowns vanished. Galaxy maps he couldn't understand. Hyper-hops meant nothing to him. But disgusting – disgusting he knew about.

'Ere!' he bellowed. 'Who you callin' disgustin'?'

'You, you undercover nincompoop!'

'Right! That's it.' It was Masher's turn to be indignant now, and it was the one subject he was good at.

Placing BrainBox on the ground, he lifted his right leg. 'I ain't standin' for that, Ros. I'm gonna put my foot down!'

'Waaggh!' screeched the computer.

'Masher! No!' yelled Ros.

'This called me a disgusting earth-creature,' said Masher, his foot still hovering above Brain-Box, 'I don't fink that's very nice.'

'No, it wasn't,' cooed Ros. She laid a hand on Masher's arm. 'But don't mash it, Masher. Please.'

With the care of a circus performer putting herself at the mercy of an elephant, Ros bent down and lifted BrainBox from beneath Masher's foot.

'Thank you,' said BrainBox.

The computer's circuits were whizzing round in circles. Could it be that, for the first time since they had rolled off the assembly line at the Sigma–6 Computer Company, they had made a serious miscalculation?

'Lewis?' purred BrainBox. 'Old chum. Don't you remember me? Your faithful pal, BrainBox? Don't you, Lewis?'

'It's calling me names again, Ros.'

'But I'm not!' squawked BrainBox. 'You *are* Lewis! Aren't you?'

'My name's McTurk,' said Masher. 'Uvverwise known as Masher on account of how . . .' he lifted a massive fist in front of BrainBox's vision sensors, '. . . I like mashing things. Let me mash it, Ros.'

'No,' said Ros sharply. There was a mystery here that needed clearing up. 'Who is Lewis?' she asked BrainBox.

BrainBox answered at once. This was a question, and questions were what computers were designed to answer. The General had said so himself. 'Lewis, Gizzmo. Agent 071349, Sigma–6 Secret Service.'

'Secret Service! You mean an undercover agent? What does he look like? One of us?'

'He does now. With my transformation tablets he can look like anything he wants.'

She'd guessed as much! 'You mean the new kid we nicked . . . I mean, we borrowed you off – he's an alien?'

'Correct.'

'And . . . he can make himself look like anything he wants if he takes one of these wajjermecallits . . .'

'Transformation tablets. Yes.'

'Even . . .' Ros saw it all now. '. . . a flea?'

'Anything,' said BrainBox. 'All down to me of course. Another of my cosmic wonder-inventions.'

'In that case,' said Ros, 'your cosmic wonder-invention hasn't done him a lot of good.'

'Pardon?' said BrainBox, offended. 'Do one's aural sensors deceive one? Did you say that one of my inventions, *my* inventions, is a failure?'

73

'Sure did,' said Ros, her last view of Stony still fresh in her mind. 'The last time I saw your mate he was about to be gazonked all over the wall by a maths book.'

Incompetent fools! She was surrounded by incompetent fools!

Stony looked up at the sight of her school caretaker, dangling from the St Arthur's sign-board. Pathetic. The man couldn't stop a tortoise escaping from its shell. He had to go.

'Dobson,' she screamed at the dangling caretaker, 'you are suspended!'

With a terrible ripping sound, Dobson's coat tore in two and he fell to the ground. It was the final straw. He'd just snapped his mop and almost kicked the bucket.

'No, I'm not!' he shouted. 'I resign!'

Gizzmo, though, had no choice but to hang in there.

As the star thugs' commanding officer moved away from the training camp and began increasing her speed, Gizzmo tightened his grip. It seemed he was being carried towards the tall building on which they'd landed earlier that day.

He burrowed down into Stony's hairdo. Things hadn't worked out quite the way he'd planned, but nobody could say he wasn't getting ahead.

'Gazonked?' said BrainBox. Extensive as the computer's memory banks were, even they had no record of such a word.

'Gazonked,' repeated Ros. 'Splattered. Splodged. Squidged. Flattened.'

'You mean . . .' said BrainBox, 'Gizzmo's been . . . .'

'Mashed,' said Masher.

'Uggh,' said BrainBox, turning a sickly shade of green.

The gazonking of Gizzmo was serious news. Without him a return to Sigma–6 was impossible. Being a mega-brain was fine as far as it went but, without useful things like arms and legs, that wasn't going to be very far.

Somebody has to take Gizzmo's place, reasoned BrainBox. Somebody with arms and legs. Somebody . . . or some bodies . . . like the two earth-creatures.

Yes! The problem was solved! If these two – with suitable assistance, of course – could be persuaded to fly the Space-Hopper back to Sigma–6, all would be wonderful.

The General would have a couple of earth-creatures to tell him everything he needed to know – and oneself, BrainBox, would get all the credit! Perfect!

The computer glowed with pleasure. 'So, what else would you like to know?' it said to Ros and Masher.

'Where's your spaceship?' said Ros.

'Is that all?' replied BrainBox. 'Wouldn't you like to know . . . how to fly it?'

* * *

Gizzmo hadn't had such a bumpy ride since he'd tried the Whirling Jelly-Legger on a day out at the Sigma–6 Whizzny World.

He'd been thrown this way and that as the star thugs' commanding officer had charged along the street and thundered around corners. Now, it was only with the greatest effort he managed to hang on as she screeched to a halt and looked up.

Gizzmo peeped out. He could see the building he'd landed his Space-Hopper on. Halfway up he could see a gap, through which he could see some stairs. And climbing those stairs were the two escaping star thugs!

With a snarl of 'Gotcha!' the star thugs' commanding officer started running again.

Ros led the way up the final flight of stairs.

'Why don't the lifts in these places ever work?' she gasped.

'Cos we keep busting 'em, Ros,' said Masher.

They continued climbing. 'At last!' said Ros. The stairs went no further. They were at the top. Forget UFOs. Ros was about to be the first person in history to see an IFO. An *Identified* Flying Object!

She led the way out onto the top deck of the multi-storey car park. Out onto the (thanks to Lionel A. Fothergill) wide, open, completely empty, totally UFO-IFO-or any-other-FO-free top deck of the council's multi-storey car park.

'Masher,' she said coldly, 'I think you were right.' She rapped BrainBox on the top with her knuckles. 'The time has come to put your foot down.'

Stony's feet were going up and up, higher and higher, faster and faster.

Seeing the two truants had given her renewed energy for the chase. She had always prided herself that her school was a happy school, a pleasant school, a school to which her pupils came every morning with joy in their hearts and a spring in their step – not a school that pupils ran away from with joy in their hearts and a spring in their step.

Rosalind Price and the numbskull McTurk were going to find that out. And soon.

She didn't bother trying the lift. It never worked. With a spring in her own step, Stony began to bound up the car-park stairs two at a time.

In next to no time she was at the top and bursting out into the fresh breeze and open spaces of the top deck.

As he felt the star thugs' commanding officer come to a halt, Gizzmo forced his spindly legs up to the summit of Stony's hairdo.

What could he see?

Well!

He could see the sun.

He could see the sky.

He could see the two deserters!

He could see BrainBox, being held tightly by the Masher-thug.

He could hear them, too. He could hear the Ros-thug shouting, 'It's Stony! Run for it!'

He could see them turning.

He could see them getting further away.

He could feel the star thugs' commanding officer picking up speed again.

Gizzmo thought quickly. What should he do? Stay where he was and hope that he'd be able to escape before his flea transformation tablet wore off, recover the rest of his tablets from the Stony-officer's kit-bag, rescue BrainBox and get back here to his Space-Hopper before flying back to Sigma–6 again?

Or jump now? Although he couldn't actually see his Space-Hopper, this was definitely where they'd landed. It must be around somewhere.

Gizzmo jumped.

Well! That was another thing he'd discovered about being an earth-flea. You landed on your feet.

Up ahead, Gizzmo caught a final glimpse of the two deserters disappearing through a gap in the wall, quickly followed by their command-ing officer.

Alone, at last.

Now, where was his Space-Hopper?

Bb-d . . . Bbb-dng. Bb-dlob.

Gizzmo found he could hardly move. His legs were feeling funny. Was it tiredness? No, he realized. The flea transformation tablet was start-ing to wear off.

This time, though, there seemed to be noises as well as feelings.

He heard a low whining noise, followed by a dull

thud. Then a click. Then slow clomp-clomp sounds.

He realized then that he wasn't making the noises. They were coming from behind him.

Gizzmo swung himself round. He was getting bigger again. Things that had looked enormous to him as an earth-flea, were no longer quite so large.

A matchstick nearby was looking more like a matchstick and less like a log. A stone was looking more like a stone and less like the side of a mountain. And, in front of him, the pair of boots he was staring at were looking more like . . . a pair of boots.

Boots?

Yes, boots. Black boots.

Joined to a pair of legs, realized Gizzmo as he continued growing back to his normal size. Two legs. Blue legs. And a blue body, with shiny buttons. And a head. And a hat. A big pointed hat, with a shiny badge on the front.

As the transformation tablet wore off completely and Gizzmo returned to his Sigma–6 shape, the head spoke.

'Hello, hello, hello,' it said. 'What's all this then?'

12

The Long Arms Of The Law

Gizzmo gulped. In front of him, the earthling dressed in blue was looking very serious. Very serious indeed.

'I have reason to believe,' it was saying, 'that you might be able to help me with my enquiries.'

'M-m-m-me?' stammered Gizzmo.

'Yes, you.'

'Wh-wh-why?'

'I have reason to believe that you are a secret agent from the planet Sigma–6.'

Gizzmo's heart sank. His cover had been blown! But how?

Before he could run for it, the earth-creature reached out and clutched him tightly. Then it began to make a peculiar ho-ho-ho-ing noise. Its shoulders began to shake. In the middle of its ho-ho-ho-ing it spoke again.

'Had you fooled there, Lewis. Good one, eh?'

'Lewis? Lewis? The earth-creature knew his name as well! How? And how come it was talking Sigmatian?

'These transformation tablets work a treat. I found a whole box of these in the stores. 'Earth-policemen' they are.'

Transformation tablets? Speaking Sigmatian?

Who . . . Gizzmo suddenly fell in. 'General?' he said. 'Is that you?'

'Absolutely,' beamed the face beneath the pointed hat. 'After your report about the star thugs, Lewis, I thought I'd better come and have a look for myself.'

'G-golly,' said Gizzmo. 'That was brave, General.'

'True, true. But then us Generals are prepared to sacrifice ourselves for our planet, Lewis. Besides, I've brought all the other secret agents with me.' He pointed a finger into the sky. 'Up there in orbit they are, just waiting for my call. Any hint of trouble . . .' he waggled the little speaker attached to his lapel, 'and I'll have 'em down here sharpish to rescue me. And you, of course,' added The General as an afterthought. 'Now then, Lewis, what more have you got to tell me? Did you get into the star thugs' training camp?'

'Yes, General,' said Gizzmo.

'Did you find out anything? Are they as dangerous as they look?'

'Yes sir, General. Definitely,' said Gizzmo. He was about to describe what it had been like to have the star thugs commanding officer doing her best to flatten him with a book when The General stopped him.

'Better swallow another transformation tablet, Lewis. Before you get spotted.'

'Ah,' said Gizzmo. 'I . . . ha-ha . . . er . . . I haven't got them, sir.'

The General gave him an icy stare. 'I hope you haven't lost them, Lewis.'

'Lost them, sir? No, sir!' Well, it was true – he knew just where they were. 'They're . . . er . . . in a safe place, General.'

The General sniffed doubtfully, then dug into the pocket of his earth-policeman's uniform. 'Here. You'd better take one of these.'

Gizzmo gulped down one of The General's transformation tablets. A minute later he, too, had taken on the form of an earth-policeman with an identical uniform to that of The General. Well, almost identical, noticed Gizzmo. For some reason The General's uniform had three funny stripes on its arms. He was about to mention this fact but The General had started talking again.

'So they're dangerous, you say?'

'Very.'

'Nasty,' said The General. 'Very nasty. What's your opinion, BrainBox?'

Gizzmo gave a little laugh.

'Where is BrainBox?' demanded The General. 'You haven't lost BrainBox as well I hope?'

'No, sir!' It was true, he hadn't. 'No General, BrainBox is . . . er . . . not with me, but . . . er . . . not far away.'

'Lewis,' growled The General, 'you haven't got your transformation tablets and you haven't got your computer. You'll be telling me next your Space-Hopper's disappeared.'

Gizzmo snapped to attention. This was his chance to restore The General's faith in him. If there was one thing he hadn't lost it was his Space-Hopper!

Now, where was it? He looked around.

There, of course, where he'd left it.

82

'One Space-Hopper, sir!' he said, pointing to the gleaming Rolls-Royce parked a short distance behind The General. 'All present and correct!'

'Your Space-Hopper?' said The General slowly. '*Your* Space-Hopper? That's *my* Space-Hopper, Lewis! I've just landed in that.'

'Y-y-yours?' said Gizzmo. His heart sank. They'd got his Space-Hopper too?

'Lewis,' growled The General. His face had taken on the appearance of a stormy night on the planet ThunderGuts Major. 'You have some explaining to do . . .'

'So,' said The General, after Gizzmo had told him everything that had happened, 'let me see if I've got this right. Since landing on this planet you've managed to lose a Mark 2 Whereami Orbital Outing Space-Hopper, you've allowed BrainBox to be captured by these Ros and Masher star thugs, and your transformation tablets to be snaffled by their commanding officer. Right?'

'Yes, General,' said Gizzmo.

'And this commanding officer is after the star thugs?'

'Yes, General.'

'So if she catches them she'll have BrainBox and all our secrets?'

'Yes, General.'

'Brilliant!'

'Do you really think so, General?'

'No I do not!' yelled The General. 'I think it's a complete mess, Lewis, and if it isn't cleared up, Lewis, I think you're going to spend the rest of your career working down the Sigma–6 salt moons, Lewis, that's what I think!'

Gizzmo hung his head in shame. 'Sorry, General.'

'This Stony-officer has got to be stopped,' snapped The General. 'BrainBox has got to be recovered.'

'Yes, sir. How, sir?'

'Simple. I call down the rest of the agents, and between us we grab her and pack her off to somewhere like Outer Moongolia for a few billion years.'

'She might be difficult to overpower, General.'

'Nonsense,' scoffed The General. 'Finding her will be the hard bit. I suppose you've lost her as well as everything else?'

At last, thought Gizzmo. A chance to impress. 'No, General,' he said crisply, 'I have not. They went this way.'

Gizzmo led the way across to the hole in the wall he'd seen the Ros-thug and the Masher-thug go through before being followed by the Stony-officer.

Apart from the big boots, his police-body was quite comfortable. One thing was bothering him, though.

'General,' he hissed as they stepped through the hole and out on to a concrete walkway, 'what exactly is an earth-policeman?'

'Silly question, Lewis,' replied The General. 'An earth-policeman is ... well I never! A moving staircase.'

They'd reached the end of the walkway to find

the most amazing sight. Far below them was a brightly-lit underground cave. And leading from it, two moving staircases, one going down into the cave and the other coming up.

'What do we do now?' asked Gizzmo.

'We boldly go where no Sigmatian has gone before, Lewis,' said The General. He boldly stepped on to the staircase going down.

Gizzmo took a deep breath and followed.

'You were going to tell me what an earth-policeman is, sir,' he whispered in The General's ear.

'Ah . . .' said The General. 'Well . . . an earth-policeman is . . . er . . . ah . . . well . . .'

'You do know, don't you General?'

'Of course I do, Lewis. An earth-policeman is . . . er . . .'

He was interrupted by a happy cry from the staircase going up. 'Good afternoon!'

They both looked across at the earth-creature who was just passing them. He seemed to be smiling, although the fuzzy black line on his top lip made it difficult to tell. He waved and called out again, 'Good afternoon, fellow believers in the ways of right!'

'There you are, Lewis,' said The General as the staircase took the cheerful earth-creature upwards and onwards, 'an earth-policeman is . . . er . . . a fellow who . . . er . . . believes he's going the right way.'

Gizzmo didn't argue. Right way or not, they were about to reach the floor of the underground cave.

Lionel A. Fothergill stepped brightly off the escalator as it reached the top level of the multi-storey car park. What a brilliant day it had been! How he was going to last until it was time to go home and tell his mum all about it, he really didn't know.

He day-dreamed happily along the walkway. Lionel A. Fothergill, suspicious vehicle detector extraordinaire. From this day forward his name would be known throughout the town!

Perhaps the word has got round already, thought Lionel, remembering the two policemen he'd just seen on the down escalator. Had they heard the news and been unable to resist coming up here to look for themselves?

Who could blame them? After all, this place was likely to become a tourist attraction. 'This,' guides would tell endless streams of goggling visitors, 'is where Lionel A. Fothergill spotted an illegally parked Rolls-Royce ...'

He reached the end of the walkway and turned to look out on the scene of his triumph.

'... an illegally parked Rolls-Royce TWICE!!!'

Lionel rubbed his eyes. Was he seeing things? Surely even the daftest owner wouldn't bring the same car back to the same spot from which it had just been removed by a vigilant Fothergill?

He scorched across to where the car stood. No tax disc. No number plate. No sticky whatsit.

One daft owner.

One-and-only Lionel A. Fothergill does it again!

Or does he? Maybe that's where the two policemen were going, thought Lionel – to arrange for this car to be towed away again.

On the other hand, maybe they weren't. Maybe

they hadn't been smart enough to spot it. It took a shrewd eye, after all. Still, as fellow believers in the ways of right and all that stuff he had to give them their chance.

Yes, thought Lionel, in the circumstances there was only one thing he could do.

Stand guard until they came back.

13
Gizzmo On The Beat

Stony was on guard too. But standing she wasn't.

She was sitting, comfortably, at a small round table. In front of her was a steaming cup of coffee. The headmistress opened her handbag, took out her box of sugar lumps, and popped one of the little cubes into her cup. Stirring her coffee slowly, she looked out across the shopping mall. She gazed beyond the clear window of one shop in particular, and smiled happily.

She'd got them now.

They were fools to have thought they could escape her. A wise head would always win the day, and that's what she had — a wise head. Lesser mortals, Stony told herself, would have chased down the escalator after Rosalind Price and her idiot accomplice McTurk. She, on the other hand, had used her head and simply looked down from above to see precisely where they went.

Only then had she come down, bought herself a coffee at the shopping mall's island café, selected a table that would give her a perfect view of the shop in which her escaped pupils were hiding, and sat down to enjoy a leisurely wait.

She expected to have time enough both to enjoy her coffee and invent a suitable punishment.

Stony had had her hair done at Clippers before

now, and – like McTurk and Miss Price – they weren't the fastest of workers.

Inside Clippers – the hairdresser for the 90s style – Ros was not getting her usual enjoyment out of having her hair done.

'You,' she hissed at BrainBox, 'I've a good mind to put you in one of those sinks and turn the cold tap on. You said you were leading us to your spaceship. So where was it?'

BrainBox turned an embarrassed pink. 'One has been thinking about that and one can only put it down to a minor lapse of memory. One hasn't been well, you know.'

'We nearly got caught because of you. If it hadn't been for me having the bright idea of coming in here, you'd be in Stony's hands now.'

'True. One is not unappreciative. And to prove it, one *will* lead you to one's Space-Hopper.'

'How?' hissed Ros. 'What makes you think you can find it next time.'

'One has the technology,' said BrainBox. A small antenna glided silently out of the computer's top.

'What are you doing?'

'Engaging WOOSH detection circuitry,' said BrainBox. 'Scanning immediate vicinity for WOOSH whereabouts.' The computer blinked steadily for a few seconds as the antenna swivelled round. Suddenly it stopped. 'WOOOSH detected,' announced BrainBox.

'You sure?' said Ros. 'You're really sure?'

'Positive. Only a WOOSH sends out the signals

89

one is now receiving. One can take you straight to it. Now, if you wish.'

Ros brightened. Maybe things hadn't worked out so bad. After all, they'd given Stony the slip, hadn't they? There was plenty of time to go and find the UFO. And after having her hair done she'd look even better on the Nine O'Clock News.

'When I'm done,' she said to BrainBox.

Ros settled back as the hairdryer over her head began pumping out heat. Her sense of well-being was virtually complete. Only a little cry of fear from the person in the next chair disturbed her.

As the adjacent hairdryer throbbed into life she turned and gave her neighbour a withering look. 'Don't worry, Masher,' she said scornfully, 'it doesn't hurt.'

Masher felt afraid. And daft.

Is it all worth it? he asked himself. It was a tricky question, so he didn't get an answer.

But he did find himself wondering. Ros was ace all right, but would she ever think he was ace as well? Did she ever think of him the way he thought of her? Did she ever consider his feelings?

If this episode was anything to judge by it didn't seem like it.

'Stony won't spot us in here!' she'd said as they'd dashed through the doors. 'Us?' he'd said. 'Whajjer mean us, Ros?'

Now he knew. He'd had his hair washed for the first time since he was christened. And now this!

Masher pulled the pink-and-white flowered smock up to his chin. He closed his eyes. Above

90

them, the heat from the dryer began to fight its way through his crew-cut.

Stony sipped her coffee thoughtfully. A tiny cloud had drifted across her happy mind. There was a flaw in her plan.

She would see Rosalind Price and Dudley McTurk when they finally came out of Clippers. But would she be able to catch them? One of them, certainly, but both of them? What if they separated and dashed off in different directions? Stony found the thought of either of them escaping from her very painful.

What she needed was some help. Another pair of hands. Or arms. Long arms. Ideally, the long arms of the law . . .

Stony leapt to her feet. Wonderful! Whoever said they were never around when you wanted them?

'Excuse me!' she yelled at the senior of the two policemen she'd just spotted strolling by, 'Sergeant!'

'Oh, no!' hissed Gizzmo, 'it's her!'

'Who?' hissed The General.

'The star thugs' commanding officer! She must have recognized us!'

'Impossible, Lewis. This earth-policeman disguise is perfect. She must want to know the right way to somewhere. This is our chance to find out where.'

Gizzmo wasn't so sure about that. He was start-

91

ing to suspect that there was something about being an earth-policeman that was . . . well, a bit more than knowing the right way to places. As they'd walked through this underground cave, he'd noticed earth-creatures had given them nervous smiles and stepped aside to let them go by.

'But . . .' he began.

It was no good. The General had taken a bold step round a potted plant and was already approaching Stony's table.

Gizzmo followed him over, a safe distance behind. After his experience as a flea, he wanted to be well out of reach if the woman turned nasty.

'Yes, madam?' said The General. 'How can I be of assistance?'

'Sergeant, I need your help.'

'Yes, madam,' said The General, 'you want to know the right way, correct?'

'The right way?'

'The right way.'

'The right way to what?'

'Er . . .' stammered The General, 'to . . . er . . . the way . . . er . . . that is . . . er . . . the right . . . er . . . way.'

'I don't want to know the right way to anywhere,' snapped Stony. 'Quite the opposite. I want you to catch a pair who have gone the wrong way!'

'Ah,' said The General, nodding seriously. He turned to look at Gizzmo. 'Got that Lewis? The wrong way.'

'A pair of habitual truants,' said Stony.

'Truants?'

'Truants.'

The General nodded again. 'Ah. Truants.'

'Yes, truants!' yelled Stony. She couldn't recall any past pupils of St Arthur's having gone on to join the police force, but the man in front of her was certainly giving every impression of having received a St Arthur's education. 'Absconders! Runaways! Deserters!'

'Ah, deserters!' said The General. He gave Gizzmo a look which said, 'There you are Lewis, follow your General and you'll be all right.'

'Truants, deserters, call them what you will,' said Stony. She gestured to the two empty chairs at her table. 'Sit down and I will describe them to you.'

Gizzmo waited until The General sat down next to the star thugs' commanding officer, then sat down himself. So, an earth-policeman was expected to catch earth-creatures who had gone the wrong way? Was that right? Had their disguises fooled the star thugs' Commanding Officer so much that she was actually asking them to help do her dirty work?

The Stony-person's next words confirmed this suspicion. 'Their names are Price and McTurk,' she said. 'Rosalind Price and Dudley McTurk. They have escaped from my training establishment.'

'*The* deserters,' said The General, with another smug look at Gizzmo.

Stony's eyes widened. Perhaps she'd been too hasty in her judgement. Perhaps behind this bumbling exterior there lay an incisive mind. 'You know about them?' she said, giving The General a warm smile. 'Already? How jolly clever of you.'

93

The General straightened his tie. 'We have our methods, madam.'

'Good,' said Stony. 'Then I trust you will catch these two for me. Because they are a positively mutinous pair. This afternoon, this very afternoon, they incited a mass desertion . . .' The headmistress whacked the table with her hand. '. . . And when I get hold of them they will get a rocket the like of which they have never seen before!'

Rocket! thought Gizzmo. Was she planning to launch the Ros-thug and the Masher-thug into outer space as a punishment?

'They will see stars, believe you me!' yelled Stony.

Yes, she was! She was going to make an example of the two deserters by sending them to the front line! The invasion must be imminent!

Desperately, Gizzmo looked at The General expecting to see that he, too, had seen the seriousness of the situation.

But he obviously hadn't. He seemed to be concentrating completely on the star thugs' commanding officer.

She was smiling again. 'Would you like me to help you in your enquiries?' she was saying.

'How?' said The General. 'Dear lady.'

'By telling you where Price and McTurk are hiding out?'

Gizzmo leapt from his seat with excitement. 'You know?'

Stony nodded, then pointed. 'They're in there,' she said.

Gizzmo looked across to the window of Clippers.

The sight stunned him. Behind the window, a row of earth-creatures seemed to be sitting, each with a peculiar machine over their heads.

Were the two star thugs amongst them? And, if they were, what were the machines doing to them?

What was this place?

'In . . . in there?' stammered Gizzmo. 'Doing what?'

'Having their heads tested, I hope,' answered Stony with a cold laugh.

Heads tested? Gizzmo looked again. Spread across the big window was another sign.

'Wash 'n Cut,' said the sign. 'Instant Service.'

Oh, no! The full enormity of the situation came to Gizzmo in a flash. The Ros-thug and the Masher-thug had already been caught. They'd been caught and sent into that place.

And now, while the star thugs' commanding officer waited, they were being washed and cut!

That's what the head machines were for – the star thugs were being brain-washed!

What a way to keep your troops under control!

But then another thought struck Gizzmo. If the two star thugs had their memories cut and washed, how would they be able to tell him and The General about their invasion plans? They wouldn't! The Stony-officer had thought of everything. The fiend!

He had to get the star thugs out. But how?

A diversion, that's what was needed. That's how they'd escaped from their Commanding Officer's clutches in the first place. But Gizzmo wasn't going to become a flea again. Not likely.

And, anyway, his box of transformation tablets were out of reach, locked in the dreaded Stony-officer's kit-bag . . .

Stony was feeling wonderful. Not only did she have Rosalind Price and the numbskull McTurk under surveillance, she now had two policemen to help her out.

This called for a small celebration. A little treat. What? A second sugar lump in her coffee, that was what. She knew they were bad for her, but this was a special event.

She opened her handbag.

At the sight of the Stony woman opening her kit-bag, Gizzmo knew it was now or never.

'They're coming out!' he yelled, slamming his hands on the table and stamping his feet. He couldn't have made a bigger crash and a wallop if he'd been a bolt of spacestorm thunder-and-frightening.

Stony reacted instantly. 'Where?' she snapped, leaping to her feet.

The General jumped up as well. 'What? Who? Where?'

It was just what Gizzmo had hoped would happen. As the other two looked over towards the brain-washing laboratory, he reached out and plucked his box of transformation tablets from the Stony-officer's kit-bag.

He didn't have time to be choosy.

He just picked out the first one he laid hands on.

If this doesn't cause a diversion, nothing will,

thought Gizzmo as he dropped the transformation tablet into Stony's coffee cup.

'False alarm,' said Stony, sitting down again. 'I can still see them sitting in there.'

She turned to The General. 'Junior, is he?' she said, nodding towards Gizzmo.

'Very,' said The General.

He gazed into Stony's eyes. Can't see what Lewis has been making so much fuss about, he thought. Perfectly delightful creature, he thought.

And then Stony took another sip of her coffee.

14
The Great Escape

At first, things seemed to Gizzmo to be happening in slow motion.

He saw the star thugs' commanding officer lift her cup to her lips.

He saw her take a sip of her bubbly drink.

He saw her put her cup down again.

Then, just as Gizzmo was starting to think that the transformation tablet was going to have no effect at all, things speeded up dramatically.

One moment the Stony-officer was looking at The General.

The next, in a blur of movement, she was leaping into his lap, flinging her arms around his neck and then, with a cry of 'Oh, you gorgeous creature, you!' pressing her lips all over his face with loud slurp-plonking noises.

The pace hotted up even more then.

'Wob . . . gelloff . . . gubble . . .' The General spluttered.

Slurp-plonk, slurp-plonk came the sounds of the Stony-officer's lips landing on The General's face.

'I . . . wob . . . ooh . . .'

'You . . .' slurp-plonk. 'Wonderful . . .' slurp-plonk. 'Man . . .' slurp-plonk.

The General broke free for an instant. 'Madam! Really!' he cried out.

'Yes, really!' hollered Stony and launched herself at The General again.

Ssslllurpp-pppplonk!

With a nasty crack the chair gave up trying to support a large Sigma–6 General and an even larger earth-headmistress and collapsed.

In summary, then, it was a real cracker of a diversion.

Gizzmo leapt up and ran.

Should he have tried to rescue The General first? No. After all, as The General had said himself, 'Us Generals are prepared to sacrifice ourselves for our planet, Lewis.'

As he ran, he looked back. Sacrificing himself was certainly what The General seemed to be doing. The Stony-woman had now got him in a form of neck-lock probably known only to black-belt star thugs' commanding officers.

Gizzmo, the secret agent told himself, you've got to do this on your own.

He put his head down and charged through the door of the brain-washing laboratory.

As far as The General was concerned, there was good news and bad news.

The good news was that the star thugs' commanding officer was no longer slurp-plonking all over his face.

The bad news was that she now had his head in a grip that would have won a submission from the all-Sigma crater-wrestling champion and had started nibbling his ear.

The General twisted his head in an attempt to escape. The move was a partial success. It didn't stop the nibbling, but it did cause his nose to collide with the intercom unit in his lapel.

It crackled into life.

'Hello,' said a voice. 'Sigma Force to General. Come in, General.'

'Help!' croaked The General. 'Emergency! Scramble all units! Aaghh!'

He got no further before his lips were squashed beneath another wave of slurp-plonking.

Gizzmo came straight to the point.

'Run for it!' he yelled to everybody in the brainwashing laboratory. 'Quick!'

The sight of a policeman charging through the door had an immediate effect on both Ros and Masher.

Masher hid his eyes and shouted, 'It wasn't me! I didn't do it!'

Ros, on the other hand, pointed at Masher and shouted, 'It was him! He did it!'

Gizzmo didn't have time for all this. Quickly he snatched BrainBox from Masher's hands. 'Brain-Box!' he yelled at the computer, 'It's me, Gizzmo! Tell them it's me!'

'It's him,' said BrainBox. 'It's definitely him. I'd know those vibes anywhere.'

'Who?' said Ros.

'Lewis,' said BrainBox. 'My fellow traveller.'

'The one who turned into a flea?' said Ros. She pulled her head out from beneath the hairdryer and looked up at Gizzmo. 'How'd you get away from Stony?'

'It's a hair-raising story,' said Gizzmo. 'But we

haven't got time. If you don't get a move on she'll be in here. So come on!'

Ros didn't need telling twice. Even as one of the other customers shouted, 'A bomb! It must be a bomb!' and everybody dived for cover, she was on the move.

'Come on!' yelled Gizzmo at Masher. 'Do you want your brain washed? Run for it!'

Masher lumbered out from beneath his hairdryer. Questions like: why was this policeman who was a flea from outer space telling him to run before his brain was washed, and how did he think they'd be able to hang it on the line even if it had been? would have to wait. Ros was running, so he would too.

With more cries of 'Bomb! It must be a bomb!' ringing in their ears, they all dashed out of the hairdresser's and into the heart of the shopping mall.

The General had just managed to loosen his head a little more as the cries of 'Bomb! It must be a bomb!' reached the island café.

Bomb? Bomb?

All around him earth creatures were diving to the floor as the shouting increased.

And across the way, he could just see three others running, one with a box in his hands.

So that's why he'd been flung to the ground by this Stony-woman! To be saved from a bomb! How could he have misjudged her so?

'Cancel that order!' he snapped into the intercom.

'Pardon, General?'

101

'Unscramble! Await further orders!'

He wrenched his ear from between the Stony-officer's teeth and forced his neck back round so that he was facing her.

This wonderful woman, this fellow commanding officer, had saved him from a bomb!

'Dear, dear lady,' he whispered tenderly, 'how can I ever thank you?'

'I will tell you later, dear man,' she said breathlessly. 'First things first.'

Sluuuurrrrrrpppppppppppplonnnkkkkkkk!

He'd done it! He'd freed them! BrainBox, the Ros-thug, the Masher-thug, his transformation tablets now back in his pocket – all of them!

Well, nearly all of them. Pity about The General.

As they leapt onto the moving staircase and began to rise up towards the heavens again, Gizzmo looked back down on the scene below.

The General was struggling to his feet now, in spite of the fact that the star thugs' commanding officer seemed to be trying to bite his ear off.

Peculiar thing. For all her aggression, she didn't seem to be trying to hurt him. Quite the opposite. While trying to bite his ear, she was also stroking his hair. Now she was dusting off his earth-policeman's uniform.

Whatever the transformation tablet had done to her, it hadn't made her angrier. So what had it done?

'Brilliant!'

It was the Ros-thug. She, too, Gizzmo saw, was looking down.

102

'You think so?' The girl seemed to understand what was happening.

'Absolutely. Making Stony go bananas over a policeman! How'd you do that?'

Bananas? What was she on about? Gizzmo smiled, in what he hoped was a superior, secret agent's fashion. 'Trade secret,' he said.

'Tell us. Go on,' insisted Ros.

Should he? Why not? They were all on the same side now, after all.

'I slipped her a transformation tablet,' he said.

'And that did . . . that?' It was Masher, looking, for Masher, incredibly thoughtful.

'Seems so.'

'Why? How?' asked Ros.

'Er . . . well . . .' said Gizzmo. 'I don't actually know.'

'Then why not ask the inventor?' said a voice from beneath Gizzmo's arm.

'BrainBox! I'd almost forgotten about you.'

'Obviously.'

'All right, then. What *does* happen when an earth person swallows a transformation tablet?'

The computer flickered brightly. 'Well now. Let me see. The intended function of any transformation tablet is to activate a fundamental metabolic re-arrangement of the Sigmation physiology . . .'

'Keep it simple, BrainBox,' said Ros. 'Remember Masher.'

'A transformation tablet,' sighed the computer, 'if taken by a Sigma–6 person like Lewis here, changes his body but leaves his mind alone.'

'Right,' said Gizzmo. 'But if a transformation tablet is taken by an earthling?'

103

'Like Stony,' added Ros.

'It would work in reverse,' said BrainBox.

'Make her run backwards, yer mean?' said Masher.

'No, I mean it would leave her body alone and change her mind.'

'Stony's never changed her mind before.'

'Well, she has now,' said Gizzmo. 'BrainBox, how would it change her mind?'

'Only too happy to work this out for you. Excuse me while I think aloud.' The computer flickered cheerfully. 'Pulse rate multiplied by corpuscular diameter multiplied by pi squared . . .'

'Well?' said Gizzmo as the computer stopped muttering. 'What's the answer?'

'The answer,' said BrainBox, 'is that precisely eight-and-a-half seconds after swallowing a transformation tablet an earth-creature will fall madly in love with the first person they clap eyes on.'

'The General,' breathed Gizzmo. 'The Stony-officer's fallen in love with The General.'

'Stars in her eyes. Yes.'

'Brilliant,' said Ros. 'Absolutely brilliant. How long does it last?'

'An hour,' said Gizzmo, with some feeling. 'Transformation tablets wear off after an hour. Don't they BrainBox?'

'One earth hour,' confirmed BrainBox. 'For a Sigmation,' the computer added.

'You mean it won't be the same for an earth creature. Does the timing work in reverse, too?'

'Sort of,' said BrainBox. 'Excuse me for a moment. Conversion factor of . . . one earth hour equals a hundred Sigma days . . . te-tum-te-tum-te-tum . . . it will wear off three months, four days, two hours and twenty-one seconds from . . . now!'

'Three months!' said Gizzmo, 'she's going to be ga-ga over The General for three months!'

'Not necessarily,' said BrainBox. 'I need to check the calculations.'

'So it might not be three months?'

'No. It could be longer.'

15

Back To The Future

Nearly there, thought Ros, as they came out once again onto the top deck of the multi-storey car park.

A few more minutes and she'd be in possession of an alien's spaceship, an alien's computer, an alien's transformation tablets and an alien himself – all of them guaranteed to secure everlasting fame and fortune for Rosalind Price.

Nearly there, thought Gizzmo,

A few more minutes and he'd be blasting off with the star thugs safely on board – all of them heading for Sigma–6 to reveal all they knew about the impending invasion.

Nearly there, thought Lionel A. Fothergill, he'd been so nearly there. A few more minutes and he'd have been claiming two Rolls-Royce bookings in a day – the highest number for a single traffic warden since records began.

But, as he saw one of the two policeman reappear in the distance – obviously returning to claim the Rolls-Royce booking for himself – he knew it was not to be. Sadly he turned and walked away.

'So, where is it?' said Ros.

Gizzmo pointed at the gleaming Rolls-Royce. Never had he seen a more welcome sight. 'There,' he said.

'That? That's a car.'

Gizzmo shook his head. 'No it's not. It's a Mark 2 Whereami Orbital Outing Space-Hopper. Isn't that so, BrainBox?'

'Correct,' said the computer.

'I don't believe it,' said Ros. 'Not until . . . I see inside.'

'Of course,' said Gizzmo. 'Open the door if you would, BrainBox.'

BrainBox's antenna wiggled slightly and at once the door of the Space-Hopper swung smoothly open.

'Wow!' said Ros, as she looked inside. 'Fantastic! And you came all the way from Sigma–6 in this?'

Gizzmo nodded. 'Plenty of room for four, as you can see. You'll both be quite comfortable on the journey. It doesn't take that long.'

'Journey?' said Ros. 'What journey?'

'The journey back to Sigma–6,' Gizzmo said. 'You're free now. You're coming with us. Both of you.'

'What?' said Masher. 'What's he on about, Ros? I don't wanna go on no journey.'

'Don't worry, Masher. We're not going anywhere.'

'But . . .' said Gizzmo, 'you must. We need you.'

Ros smiled. 'Not as much as we need you, Gizzmo.'

'Right!' said Gizzmo. 'That's what I'm saying. You need us to escape from your training camp, and we need you to tell us about the invasion plans.'

'Invasion? What invasion?'

'The star thugs invasion, of course!'

'Star thugs?'

'Star thugs!' yelled Gizzmo. Why were they being so difficult after all he'd done for them?

'We saw your training camp as we landed,' he said. 'We saw your sign-board.' He pointed down at the notice board they'd seen earlier on that day. 'Star thugs High School, see? You can't fool us. We know what you are. They can't fool us, can they BrainBox?'

'Not possible,' said the computer.

'We know what a High School is, don't we BrainBox?'

'Affirmative.'

'Tell them, BrainBox. Prove to them we know what a High School is.'

'A place for training and education . . .'

'See?'

'. . . of young people,' continued the computer. 'Main subjects studied: reading, writing, mathematics . . .'

'And space travel,' interrupted Gizzmo, 'and computer-assisted alien-zapping weapons training, and all about strong-arm astronauts and . . .'

'Negative,' said BrainBox. 'No such subjects on record.'

'What?'

'High School studies do not include those subjects.'

'Invasion tactics, then.'

'Negative.'

'Negative? Negative? What do you mean, negative?'

'Subjects taught at High School do not, definitely do not, never have included those stated. That sort of negative.'

'BrainBox!' cried Gizzmo desperately. 'That isn't right. Tell me that's not right. You're not feeling well again. Tell me you're not feeling well again.'

'Negative. Never felt better.'

'Then who . . . what . . . who . . .' he gurgled, pointing at Ros and Masher.

The computer flicked its vision sensors and gave the nearest sound possible to an electronic sniff. 'Two insignificant earth-creatures of quite pathetic intelligence Lewis, even when compared to you.'

'You mean . . . they're not trainee invaders? They're not a threat to Sigma–6?'

'No threat whatsoever.'

For a moment, Gizzmo didn't know whether to laugh or cry. Then he did. Cry.

'No threat, eh BrainBox?' snarled Ros. 'We'll see about that. Grab 'em, Masher!'

Yet again, Gizzmo found himself being grabbed by a brawny set of arms and held fast.

This time, though, he could see no chance of escape.

His cover had been blown. He'd been captured. And, worst of all, the tingling in his earth-policeman's toes told him that his transformation tablet was going to wear off pretty soon.

The situation was hopeless. Even what he could

remember from the Sigma–6 Secret Service Handbook offered little consolation.

Gizzmo closed his eyes and prayed.

That his prayer was answered, surprised Gizzmo greatly. To discover that miracles actually spoke surprised him even more. But this one certainly did.

'Unhand that policeman at once!' said the miracle sternly.

Lionel A. Fothergill had been called many things in his time, but never a miracle.

Had he not been feeling so sorry for himself he would have missed this chance too.

But he had – so, before leaving the top deck of the multi-storey car park, he'd turned and taken a last, lingering look at the Rolls-Royce he might have double-booked had the policeman not come back.

And what had he seen? That policeman, that fellow crime-fighter and unwanted vehicle apprehender, being assaulted!

At the sight of this appalling act, Lionel hadn't hesitated.

With fire in his heart, bristle in his moustache and thoughts in his mind of what his mum was going to say about this little lot, he'd dashed back across the car park and uttered the words that Gizzmo had found so miraculous.

'Unhand that policeman at once!'

Ros recovered quickly from the arrival of this strangely familiar-looking traffic warden.

'He's not a real policeman,' she cried. 'He's an alien!'

Lionel's moustache rose slightly, like a feather in a breeze. 'An alien,' he smiled.

'From Sigma–6!'

'Sigma–6.'

'Yes, Sigma–6! It's a planet in outer space. And that thing he's holding is called BrainBox! It's a computer!'

'A computer.'

'It's true,' yelled Ros. 'Tell him it's true, Masher.'

'It is,' said Masher. 'And that's . . .' he pointed at Gizzmo's Space-Hopper, '. . . a you-know, a UFO! His spaceship!'

Lionel took his hat off. What a day! His mum was never going to believe this. Two Rolls-Royces and now this. Two nutcases.

More than that, thought Lionel as he noticed the St Arthur's school uniforms they were wearing, two nutcases he'd seen before.

'I know you,' he said. 'You're Ros Price. And that's Masher McTurk.'

'LAF-a-minute!' said Ros, suddenly realizing why the traffic warden looked familiar, 'you were in the fifth form when we were second years.'

'Yes, I was. It was you who started calling me LAF-a-minute.'

'I did?'

'And you used to pinch my sandwiches,' said Lionel, his moustache quivering with emotion. 'I got told off by my mum because of you.'

'You did?'

'You told me you wanted my sandwiches to feed the poor and needy. My mum said I was the one who was poor and in need. "Poor Lionel," she said. "You need your head examined," she said. She said I shouldn't believe a word you say. And I don't!' exploded Lionel, 'I don't, I don't, I don't!'

'LAF . . . I mean Lionel,' simpered Ros, 'I am sorry.'

'I don't believe a word you say!' He looked at Gizzmo. 'An alien, indeed. He's a policeman. Anyone can see he's a policeman. So let him go,' said Lionel fiercely, 'or . . . I'm going to tell on you.'

Only as Masher released his grip did Gizzmo finally realize what had happened.

This Lionel earth-creature didn't believe the Ros and Masher pair.

He still believed that he, Gizzmo, was a real earth-policeman – just as he had when he'd waved to him and The General from the moving staircase.

Even better, the Lionel-creature was holding the Space-Hopper's door open for him and saying, 'Fair dos. It's yours.'

Brilliant!

All he had to do now was get in and take off. Quickly. The tingling in his toes was getting tinglier by the second.

Gizzmo stepped across to the Space-Hopper and

placed BrainBox inside. His ears were beginning to twitch as well now.

Hang on, he told the transformation tablet, hang on. Don't wear off yet. Another couple of seconds, that's all I need. . . .

He didn't get them.

What with all the walking he did, and the regular doses of castor oil his mum spooned into him every night before tucking him up with his teddy, Lionel A. Fothergill was a generally healthy chap. He didn't catch colds, he didn't get tummy aches, and he most definitely didn't have funny turns.

But, as he stepped across to stop the policeman getting into the Rolls-Royce, a funny turn was just what he seemed to be having.

He'd only wanted to shake the man by the hand, two guardians of the law united in one symbolic act of unity in the fight against crime.

Instead, he'd got the shakes. Before his very eyes, the policeman seemed to be changing shape. His uniform appeared to be disappearing and a shiny silver tunic was taking its place. His helmet was going too, and his round face and long legs and big boots. They were changing into . . .

'See!!' It was the girl, Ros. 'I told you he was an alien!'

Yet again, Gizzmo found that Masher's brawny arms had surrounded him and he couldn't move.

'I got him, Ros,' said Masher. 'Now what?'

'Before we use BrainBox to do our maths homework and sell the answers to the other kids at school?'

'You can't!' came an anguished cry from inside the Space-Hopper, 'one will be bored stiff! Help me, Gizzmo! Old pal!'

'Yeh, before that,' said Masher.

'And before we put Gizzmo here in a zoo, so that the whole world can come and laugh at him?'

'Yeh, before that an' all.'

Lionel A. Fothergill knew the answer. 'Before that, I go and call a *real* policeman.'

'No, you don't,' snapped Ros.

'Yes, I do,' replied Lionel firmly. 'I know my duty. Impersonation of a police officer . . .' he glared at Gizzmo, '. . . is a very serious offence.'

'No you *don't*,' repeated Ros. 'Not till you've called the newspapers and the telly cameras.' She fluffed up her hair. 'You want to be famous as well, don't you?'

Lionel didn't need long to think this over. Booking a Rolls-Royce was one thing, but as for booking an alien . . . his mum would reckon he was out of this world! 'Not half!' he said.

'Okay,' said Ros to Lionel, business-like. 'Now this is how it is. When the cameras get here, I'm first, right? They can take some pictures of me, then they can take some more pictures of me with this alien, then they can take some pictures of me with his computer, then they can take some pictures of me with his spaceship. Then they can take a picture of you.'

'What about me, Ros?' asked Masher, without loosening his grip on Gizzmo.

'Yeh, they can take a picture of you as well. If they can get you all in.'

'No, I mean, after they've taken pictures of you,

then you and this alien, then you and his computer, then you and the spaceship . . . I was thinking they could take a picture of you with me.'

'With you?'

'Yeh.'

'With you, Masher? Take a picture of me with you?'

'Yeh. Togevver, like.'

'Masher,' said Ros loftily, 'I am going to be famous. After this, I am going to be in demand. I am going to be making personal appearances, turning on the Christmas illuminations, opening bowling alleys and all that stuff. I am going to be seen at glittering occasions, Masher, walking across plush red carpets with a handsome hunk by my side.'

'Right. S'like I said. Togevver wiv me.'

'What?'

'Handsome hunk,' said Masher. 'Me.'

'You!' screeched Ros. 'You! A handsome hunk! Don't make me laugh!'

Gizzmo decided at that moment that he'd never understand earth-creatures as long as he lived.

There was the Ros-girl saying 'Don't make me laugh!' and what did she do? Start laughing.

A wide, open-mouthed laugh, pointing her finger at the Masher-boy who was holding him tight.

No, not tight. Quite loose in fact. In fact, Gizzmo suddenly realized, not touching him at all any more – apart, that was, from the big hand fishing in the pocket of his silver tunic.

Masher McTurk had never felt so upset. Ros, his beloved Ros, was laughing at him.

Deep, in a previously uncharted area of his brain, an inspiration began to bubble up.

Something to do with something that had happened recently. What was it now? Yes, that was it. The alien's transportation tablets or whatever they were. They'd had that amazing effect on Stony, so maybe. . . .

As Ros laughed on, Masher released his grip on the alien and stuck a hand in his tunic pocket instead.

He pulled out the box.

And then, with the most accurate throwing arm St Arthur's school playground had ever seen, he shot a transformation tablet straight into Ros's laughing mouth.

Gizzmo could hardly believe his luck. Another diversion was on the cards. Why he didn't know, but the Masher-boy had thrown a transformation tablet straight into the Ros-girl's mouth. She'd swallowed it!

In eight-and-a-half seconds time she would go bananas, just like the Stony-woman had.

One, two, three . . .

She would start all that slurp-plonking business with the first person she clapped eyes on.

. . . four, five . . .

Whoever that happened to be.

At that moment it was the Masher-boy. 'You!' she was yelling at him, 'do you know what you've done!' The Masher-boy was nodding.

. . . six, seven . . .

Any moment now, thought Gizzmo. He looked at the Ros-girl. She was looking at him now, and screaming, 'You and your rotten transformation tablets!'

At him! Oh, no, not at him!

. . . eight . . .

What could he do? Where could he go? She was looking at him!

. . . eight and a quarter . . .

No she wasn't. She wasn't!

She was looking at the Lionel-warden. She was looking at the Lionel-warden because the Masher-boy had grabbed him and shoved him into her so that she couldn't possibly look at anybody else.

. . . eight-and-a-half.

How odd, thought Lionel, as he found himself bumping into Ros.

And how embarrassing. Lionel had never bumped into a girl before. What would she say? 'Oy, watch it you!' probably.

Maybe something a lot worse. His moustache flinched in apprehension.

'Any time, Lionel,' purred Ros, sweetly.

'P-P-Pardon?' said a surprised Lionel. Far from being upset, she sounded almost pleased that he'd bumped into her. Or was she? Why was she advancing towards him? Why were her arms out-stretched? Why was she looking at him like that?

'Gggrrrrr. Come here, you tremendous traffic warden, you.'

Lionel didn't wait to find out. Rolls-Royces be

blowed, this was serious. There was only one person who could help him now.

'Mummeee!!!!' he yelled, 'help me, mummeee!!!'

As Lionel galloped away with Ros in hot pursuit, Gizzmo turned to Masher. The big earth-boy was still barring his way.

'We want to go home,' said Gizzmo simply.

From inside the Space-Hopper came a little cry of agreement. 'BrainBox go home. BrainBox go home.'

Masher looked from Gizzmo to BrainBox and back again. Then he nodded and stepped aside.

'Go on, then.'

Did he mean it? It wasn't a trick to grab him again? Uncertainly, Gizzmo stepped towards the Space-Hopper. 'You won't grab me?'

Masher shook his head.

'Or try and shut me up in one of your zoo places?'

'Nah,' said Masher. 'People would laugh at you.'

He glanced over to the far side of the parking area, to the gap in the wall through which he'd just seen Ros disappear, and gave a crooked smile.

'It ain't funny when people laugh at you.'

16

Home Sweet Home

Gizzmo looked at the framed certificate on the wall of his little office and stepped back.

Home Sweet Home

He sighed happily.

'Well, we made it BrainBox.'

The box on his desk winked. 'One cannot fault your logic there, Gizzmo old chum.'

'And it was a successful mission, wasn't it?'

'One would have said so, my friend.'

'I mean, we at least know now the earth-creatures aren't planning to invade us, like you thought.'

'Like *I* thought?' said BrainBox. 'Like *you* thought, you mean.'

'What do you mean, like I thought? I didn't think it at all.'

'Well if you didn't think it and I didn't think it, who did think it?'

Gizzmo gave the computer a playful tap on the top. 'You're the mega-brain. You tell me.'

BrainBox glowed. 'Easy,' said the computer. 'The General thought it.'

'The General,' said Gizzmo. 'So he did.'

He gazed out of the window at the star-spangled sky. 'I wonder how he's getting on?'

It was morning break at St Arthur's High School. Various activities were in progress.

Out by the entrance a couple of the more creative pupils were giving the school sign-board a fresh coat of paint under the watchful eye of the new caretaker.

He nodded approvingly, before moving on.

A group of older boys were playing football. One received a painful kick.

'Oy!' he yelled at his opponent, 'you dozy . . .'

The new caretaker coughed gently.

'I mean,' said the footballer hastily, 'how dozy of me to put my head on the end of your toe like that. Awfully sorry.'

With another nod of approval, the new caretaker moved on.

Perched elegantly on her usual wall, Ros Price saw none of this. She was too busy.

The big boy at her side looked up at her and grinned. 'Lionel well is he?' asked Masher. 'And his mum?'

Ros simply nodded and carried on noting down the numbers of the cars that went by in the little exercise book she'd bought especially for the purpose.

From her study window, Miss Wilhemina Hart, MA, looked out on all this with the great joy of a woman whose dream has come true.

Her school was now a model of politeness and decorum – and it was all down to the new caretaker.

What a man!

She gazed lovingly across at him, standing in the far corner of the playground. How elegant he looked in his policeman's uniform!

She watched as he popped something into his mouth.

And how brave!

How many men could take a pill every hour, on the hour, without complaining?

'There's just one thing I don't understand,' said Gizzmo. 'Why haven't all the other secret agents come back?'

'Still in orbit round the Earth, my friend,' said BrainBox. 'Awaiting further orders from The General.'

'How do you know that?'

'BigHead sent me a telegrim this morning.'

'BigHead?'

'A fellow mega-brain, slightly inferior model of course, serving on one of the orbiting Space-Hoppers. The General is refusing to answer his intercom. Either that, or the device is faulty. All they ever get from it are strange slurp-plonking noises.'

'Phew!' said Gizzmo, 'at least he's alive and well.' A thought struck him. 'But . . . if he's still there, and all the other agents are there as well, waiting for him . . .'

'Who is in charge here?' interrupted BrainBox. 'Is that what you want to know?'

'Well . . . yes.'

'Easy,' said the computer, bursting into a kaleidoscope of colour. 'You must be . . . General Gizzmo!'

THE END

A Red Fox Book

Published by Random House Children's Books
20 Vauxhall Bridge Road, London SW1V 2SA

A division of Random House UK Ltd
London Melbourne Sydney Auckland
Johannesburg and agencies throughout the world

Copyright © text Michael Coleman 1993
Cover illustration copyright © Lynne Chapman 1999

1 3 5 7 9 10 8 6 4 2

First published in Great Britain by
The Bodley Head Children's Books 1993
Published in paperback by Red Fox 1994

This Red Fox edition 1999

Printed in Norway by AIT Trondheim AS

RANDOM HOUSE UK Limited Reg. No. 954009

ISBN 0 09 926631 8

GIZZMO LEWIS

LEWIS

FAIRLY SECRET AGENT

Michael Coleman

RED FOX